APPLE SIGNATURE

Faith and the Electric Dogs

Patrick Jennings

with decorations by the author

Scholastic Inc.

New York   Toronto   London   Auckland   Sydney

A Santiago de Cuba
Espérame en el cielo, mi corazón

Muchas gracias a Elizabeth, Ruth, Betsy, Regina, and Brenda; Tracy;
Marcela and Domingo; and darling Alison.

No part of this publication may be reproduced in whole or in part, or stored in a retrieval system, or transmitted in any form or by any means, electronic, mechanical, photocopying, recording, or otherwise, without written permission of the publisher. For information regarding permission, write to Attention: Permissions Department, Scholastic Inc., 555 Broadway, New York, NY 10012.

ISBN 0-590-69769-2

12 11 10 9 8   2 3/0

Printed in the U.S.A.   40

First Scholastic paperback printing, June 1998

Contents

Prologue
Trust Me

I am about to tell you a story, dear reader, which you may have trouble believing. If it hadn't happened to me, I would probably doubt it myself. I want to reassure you, though, right here at the start, that I fully intend to tell the story as it truly happened. Still, I'm well aware that the truth may be hard for you to swallow. For example, when I tell you that I flew in a rocket ship built and piloted by a little girl named Faith, I expect that you'll grumble. Any reasonable reader would. But it *did* happen. I rode in a rocket. I would not lie about such a thing.

My story begins in San Cristóbal de las Casas, an old colonial city high up in the mountains of Chiapas, the southernmost state in Mexico. (You may wish at this point to consult an atlas or an encyclopedia. On a map of Mexico, look near the bottom.) San Cristóbal de las Casas is where I was born, where I spent my puppyhood, and where I met Faith, my master.

Puppyhood? you ask. Master? Yes, well, you see, I'm a dog. An electric dog, as a matter of fact. I suppose I should have mentioned that right off. You can call me Edison, or Eddie. That's what most people call me. Among other electric dogs I'm known as Grumph, my Bowwow name.

Encantado.

I imagine you are not used to being told stories by a dog, electric or otherwise. But then not many dogs, electric or otherwise, tell stories to people at all, probably because not many of them understand human languages. I do. I understand English (obviously), Spanish (of course, being Mexican), French, smatterings of German and Dutch, and even a little Japanese, not to mention some Mayan dialects spoken where I live.

Of course, being a dog, I can't speak these languages. They're human languages. I'm not human. I don't have a human tongue or human teeth or a human voice box. I'm a dog. I speak dog languages. My mother tongue is Bowwow. I can also speak Ruff, which is the language spoken by the well-bred house dogs of San Cristóbal de las Casas. Plus, I speak several foreign canine languages that I've picked up from dogs from other countries. These include Arf (spoken by dogs from the United States), Yap (England), Oof (the Netherlands), and Grrr (Germany). For reasons unclear to me, I have a rather unusual facility with languages.

But I'm straying now.

It's probably best that I just begin my tale without further ado. Hopefully, with time, you'll see that, at heart, I am utterly trustworthy. It's a dog thing. We can't help it.

1
Faith Rescued

The day I met Faith I had made the long, perilous journey across town to the high white cliffs south of the city, where a running stream encircles a small school. Running water is much safer, and better tasting, than the stagnant water in the city's puddles, you see.

I had perched on the stream's bank, and was just about to dive in, when I heard an odd snuffling sound coming from upstream. I crept along through the underbrush until I could see the source of the sound. Seated on the other side of the stream was a little crying girl. It was, of course, Faith.

She looked to me to be about seventy years old (in dog years, that is; in people years, about ten). Her long orange hair was bound with a blue Guatemalan headband and she wore a green cotton dress. (I have

heard people say that dogs are color-blind. Don't believe it.)

She must have sensed that I was watching her, for
she looked up and spoke to me.

"Poochy poochy poo," she said, her face brighten-
ing a little. "Mooey mooey pooey poochy poo."

Even with all of the language skills I had at my dis-
posal, I could not understand a single syllable of what
Faith said to me that day. The tongue that she spoke
was completely foreign to me.

She crooked her finger and beckoned me toward
her.

"Yessee yessee yessee wessee, you-you," she continued. "Yum-yum yummer yummy moo-moo,
widdle poochy poochy poochy pooder-doo."

I just stared at her with my tongue hanging out,
dumbfounded.

"Wootchy wootchy woo wid —" she started,
when we both heard a z-z-zinging sound. A small
object zipped just by her ear and splashed into the
stream. From behind her I heard a loud cackle from
what sounded like a small boy.

Sure enough, a moment later, a boy about Faith's
age appeared from behind a eucalyptus tree. He
puckered his lips like a fish and made a disgusting
sucking sound.

"Diego!" Faith yelled, rising to her feet.

"Diego!" Diego repeated, in a high voice.

The little monster held in his hand a wooden *tirador*.

"Leave me alone, Diego!" Faith screamed.

"Leemee halone, Diego!" Diego echoed.

Obviously he couldn't really speak English. He was merely aping whatever sounds Faith made.

Faith began crying again and Diego mocked her tears.

"Stop it!" Faith shrieked.

"Estoppit!" Diego shrieked back.

A few of his fellow young brutes appeared and joined in on the teasing. They all laughed and jeered as poor Faith cried and carried on.

I'd seen this sort of thing before. There was no telling why Diego had begun taunting Faith. Perhaps it was because she spoke English, or that she was North American, or a girl, or orange-haired. It's hard to say with boys.

"*Mira, mira,*" Diego said to his *amigos,* smirking.

He picked up a stone and placed it in the elastic band of his *tirador*.

The boys cheered and slapped one another's backs. Diego aimed the *tirador* at Faith and pulled the stone back.

Faith vainly tried to shield her body with her hands and begged Diego not to shoot.

And then, I don't know, I guess I just snapped. I'd seen all I could stand. I bounded over the stream, shot past Faith, and lunged at Diego's throat. I landed on his chest and sent him tumbling over backward onto the ground with a thump. His friends yelped, then scattered. Diego scrambled to get away, too, but when I gave him a nasty snarl, he froze.

"*Cálmate, perrito,*" he said in a wavering voice.

I continued snarling. Faith walked up beside us. She tapped her foot as she looked down at Diego squirming in the dirt.

> **Cálmate, perrito**
> *(Spanish): Calm down, little dog*

"Good dog," she said to me.

From the direction of the school I heard voices approaching. I looked up to see a crowd of children being led by several adults, all of whom looked upset. Diego's pals were in front, pointing the way.

Time to go.

I climbed off Diego and raced back to the stream. Faith followed behind.

"Wait, little poocher!" she called.

But I was already across the water and away.

2

Rescued by Faith

I didn't see Faith again until the day I was hit by a taxicab.

It's not surprising that we electric dogs are so often hit by taxicabs. Most of us spend our whole lives on the streets. Taxicabs also spend their whole lives on the streets. Sooner or later, we're bound to bump into each other. The rather unfair part of it is that the taxicab usually comes away from the collision unharmed, while that is hardly ever the case for the poor electric dog.

The day I got hit, I was doing everything right. I knew how to survive in the gutter. I was no whining whelp. I was one sharp street dog.

I remember I had been walking along Avenida General Utrilla when suddenly I was smitten by a captivating aroma from across the street. It came from Santo Domingo, the big open plaza where *indígenas* sell handicrafts. This part of town is often jammed with traffic and people. Not a safe place to cross.

But, as I said, there was this smell. And not just any smell. It was the fragrant perfume of *carnitas,* and I am most definitely a dog who loves *carnitas.*

As tempting as the smell was, I remember that I still took the time to run quickly down my safety-when-crossing checklist.

1. Look in all directions.

2. Make sure the parked cars are really parked (no brake lights, no occupants).

3. Cross mid-block (fewer cars, fewer turns, fewer surprises).

4. Listen.

5. When you decide to go, go, and go like there's no tomorrow.

I'd done all of these things, but even so, the second I stepped off the curb, I heard a screeching of tires and then a loud thud. The thud was the sound of my body being struck by a two-ton automobile. The collision sent me sailing, up over the street, over the tourists, over the fresh fruit being sold by *indígenas* on the sidewalk — over mangoes, papaya, nanchis. Then, with another thud, I landed on the stone sidewalk in a heap.

The pain was unspeakable. It was centered in my left hip but traveled throughout my body — to my

indígenas
(Spanish):
native people

carnitas
(Spanish):
roasted pork
nuggets glazed
in fat drippings

toes, my tail, my teeth. Blood oozed from a hole in my fur near my shoulder.

The taxicab never even slowed. It was out of sight before I hit the sidewalk. Several people stepped over me. Most stepped around.

I figured I was a goner, that I would die right there, in everyone's way.

Within moments I began to lose consciousness. The world became a kaleidoscope of shapes and colors.

I vaguely remember glimpsing a bright patch of orange — a shock of vivid orange, like an enormous marigold — coming toward me, getting larger. Then, for a second, my eyes focused and I could see that it was a crop of hair, orange and bound with a blue band. Below it was a freckled face.

"Poochy poochy poo," the orangehead said.

I passed out.

3
The Electric Dog

When I came to, I was in bed. I'd never been in a bed before. It was warm and soft and cozy. I liked it.

"Well, hello, widdle puppy-poo," chirped Faith, who was sitting beside me, stroking the fur between my ears. "You feeling better, little buddy?" she said.

It took a moment to remember what had happened, but then it all came back to me in a rush of pain. I lifted my head slightly off the bed. I saw that I had bandages wrapped around my upper body and that I had some kind of plaster cast on my rump.

"What kind of a dog is he, Hector?" Faith asked as she stroked me.

"Oh, no kind in particular," answered a man's voice.

I turned my head as far as I could and saw a man

sitting in a chair across the room. Hector was dark and thin with ear-length black hair. From his accent and appearance, I guessed that he was Mexican, maybe even *chiapaneco* (which, dear reader, turned out to be true).

"What do you mean?" Faith asked.

"He's just a dog, Faith," Hector said. "*Un perro corriente.* An electric dog."

She stopped stroking me and pulled her hand away.

"An electric dog?" she said, wrinkling her nose. "What do you mean?"

"It's just an expression, *mi hija,*" Hector said. "In Mexico, we call mutts 'electric dogs.'"

"Why?" Faith asked.

"Well," Hector said, "the Spanish word *corriente* means 'current,' like electrical current. But it can also mean 'cheap' or 'no good.'"

"I don't speak Spanish," Faith said.

"I know, *mi hija,* but you're learning."

"No, I'm not," Faith said seriously. "I can't learn Spanish. It's a physical impossibility."

Hector grinned.

"Are you saying this dog is no good?" Faith asked.

"No, *mi hija,*" Hector said. "I'm just saying that he's an electric dog. A mutt."

"How do you say it in Spanish again?" Faith asked.

"*Un perro corriente,*" Hector said. "Or *un perro eléctrico.* They mean the same thing."

chiapaneco
(Spanish):
from Chiapas
☆

un perro corriente
(Spanish):
an electric dog
☆

mi hija
(Spanish): my daughter; an affectionate name for a young girl

"I can't speak Spanish," Faith said.

"I know," Hector said.

"I'm going to call him Edison," Faith said. "Edison the electric dog." She smiled.

"Now, listen, *mi hija,*" Hector said. "I told you that you have to talk to your mother about that. I said I'd fix the dog up, but it's up to your mother whether or not you can keep him. Remember that. I never said you could keep him."

"Do you like your new name, widdle wupper?" Faith said to me, ignoring Hector.

"Are you listening to me?" Hector said. "Just remember, I never —"

The sound of a door opening and closing made both Faith and Hector jump. Hector actually leaped to his feet. His eyes grew wider and his movements more nervous.

"She's here!" he said, and began pacing. "Just remember. I never said! I never said!"

Faith's mother, Bernice, stepped into the room. She, too, had orange hair, though hers had dulled slightly with age. She was tall and gaunt and wore a palm-leaf hat that shaded her eyes. Her face was scrunched up as if she'd just licked a lemon.

"What *is* that stench?" she said, her shaded eyes scanning the room.

"It's Edison," Faith said. "My electric dog."

Hector sighed and slapped his forehead.

Bernice's gaze fell on me. She pulled off her hat and threw it at Hector, who fumbled to catch it. Without her hat, I could see that her eyes were green, like Faith's, but menacing.

"Isn't he cute?" Faith said, oblivious to her mother's mounting anger. "Hector says he's electric. Huh, Hector?"

Hector looked away.

Bernice threw up her hands and stomped out of the room. Hector followed after her. She said many things to him, but she spoke so quickly and loudly that I couldn't make out all of it.

But I got the gist.

Faith remained with me on the bed, and patted my head and rubbed my belly. Bless her heart.

4
Pork

And so I became an electric house dog.

The next few weeks I lived a life I'd never even dreamed of. During the day, while Faith was at school, I just lay in her bed, recuperating. That was all. I just lay there, sleeping or looking out the window. Sometimes Milagros, the family's *muchacha,* brought me kibbles, which were hard, dry, and a bit tasteless. Despite this, I ate them without complaint. Every street dog knows it's wise to eat any food within reach, so long as it hasn't spoiled.

When Faith came home from school each day, she'd sit with me, and rub me, and talk to me about how she just couldn't learn Spanish, or how Diego had made fish faces at her or shot stones at her with his *tirador.* Sometimes she'd read me stories from books she had — wonderful books like *Higglety Pigglety Pop!* and *The Amazing Bone.* Or she'd sing songs.

muchacha
(Spanish):
a young woman
or girl who is
hired as a
servant; literally,
young woman

One of my favorites was called "Rum Sum Sum." It went like this:

> *Uh rum sum sum*
> *Uh rum sum sum*
> *Gooey gooey gooey gooey rum sum sum.*
> *Uh ramby*
> *Uh ramby*
> *Gooey gooey gooey gooey rum sum sum.*

She tapped her fists together during the "rum sum sum" parts, stretched her arms way up over her head during the "ramby" parts, and made little grabbing motions during the "gooey gooey" parts. After she'd finished performing it in a normal voice and mood, she'd say, "Now, angry." Then she sang it again as if she were absolutely furious about something. After angry came sad, sleepy, happy, and scared. Or she'd sing it in character, as a tiger, or a pirate, or a ghost. My favorite was the sad pirate, all gruffness and tears.

In the evenings, after her bath, we would curl up together on the rug and she'd stroke me and sing to me and tell me she loved me so much, and I'd paw at her and lick her face and roll over on my back and she'd rub my belly.

She often told me about a place called San Francisco, California, which, despite having a Spanish name, is a city in the United States. She and Bernice used to live there before Bernice married Hector and they all moved to San Cristóbal de las Casas. She told me about an enormous red bridge called, oddly enough, the Golden Gate Bridge, which separates the San Francisco Bay and the Pacific Ocean. She told me about riding a giant frog in the children's playground. She told me about eating something called dim sum in Chinatown, and going to the aquarium in Golden Gate Park where she saw real live sharks.

I didn't really understand most of it. I'd never seen sharks or giant frogs in San Cristóbal de las Casas. But I could see it meant a lot to her, so I listened closely. Besides, she usually scratched behind my ears while she talked, and I'm a pooch who loves being scratched behind the ears.

Those were happy days.

I recuperated slowly but surely, and then one day Faith and Hector took me to the veterinarian to have the cast and bandages taken off. Soon after that I began to walk.

This meant no more days lying around eating and sleeping in bed. Hector and Faith made a little doghouse for me out on the courtyard. I must admit to being a little naive about the life of a house dog, for I remember being surprised to discover that, contrary to the rumors on the street, a house dog does not usually have his own chair at the table. Instead, I had two ceramic bowls out on the patio — one for water, one for kibbles. The family ate inside, in the dining room, overlooking the courtyard.

The first night we ate like this — they inside, I out — Milagros had prepared *carnitas*. Now, as I've clearly stated, I am definitely a *carnitas*-loving hound. The aroma alone drives me mad. And so I strode into the house, expectantly, my head held high, my tongue wagging.

"*¡Afuera!*" Bernice shrieked. "*¡Afuera!*"

I slunk back outside to my food dish. To kibbles. I crunched a few and tried to pretend they were *carnitas*. No cur has that much imagination.

I could see them all through the door, wolfing their pork, and I began to whimper a little. Only Faith stopped her feeding long enough to notice. She gave me a long, sorrowful look until her mother ordered her to close the door, which she reluctantly did.

That night, as I lay on the rug beside Faith's bed (I was no longer allowed *on* the bed — I don't think I need to say who lowered the boom), I thought about my new life. There were benefits, to be sure. Unquestionably, it was safer and meals were much more easily had. Still, a life with people was strange to me, and somewhat restrictive. I wasn't used to being told what I could and couldn't do. I was used to being pawloose and fancy-free. My own dog. I faced many indignities from people during my life on the streets, but at least I'd never had a keeper. If someone mistreated me I didn't think twice about giving them a little bite. But the hand that feeds — that's another matter entirely.

As I lay pondering all this, Faith entered the room on tiptoes.

"Ssssshh," she said.

She crouched down beside me, looked left, looked right, and then produced a grease-stained napkin from under her pajama top. She opened it to reveal a few hefty chunks of *carnitas*.

"Here you go, Eddie," she said smiling.

I scarfed them down like nobody's business and licked the napkin and Faith's fingers, too, for good measure.

She giggled and then pulled her blanket down off her bed on top of us. I snuggled up into her on the rug and soon forgot my worries and fell asleep.

5
Fetch

In the morning I was awakened by an aroma wafting from the kitchen and decided to investigate.

Milagros was there cooking eggs. Milagros is dark and broad and always wears traditional brilliant blue blouses, which she hand-embroiders herself. On the shoulder of this blouse, she'd sewn her name and surrounded it with bright yellow and pink flowers. She sang in Tzotzil while she worked.

I could smell chiles, cilantro, onions, garlic, and fresh corn tortillas.

I whined.

"¡Ay, perrito!" Milagros said.

She looked down at me and I could see pity in her eyes. She had an open, friendly face. Though she was only a teenager, she looked very grown-up.

"Mi chavi 'naj?" she asked.

I nodded and gave her my beggar face. I have

¡Ay, perrito!
(Spanish): Oh, little dog!

☆

Mi chavi 'naj?
(Tzotzil): Are you hungry?

charming, amber-colored eyes, which, combined with my creased brow — a common electric dog trait — make for an irresistible sight. I moistened my eyes and sucked in my gut. I was completely pitiable.

She looked to the left and to the right, as Faith had done the night before, and when she'd decided the coast was clear, she opened the refrigerator and withdrew a platter of the leftover *carnitas*.

"Sssshh," she said.

I stopped panting.

She gingerly plucked a particularly gooey chunk of pork from the plate and offered it to me. I seized it, swallowed it, and sighed.

Dare I whine for more? I wondered.

I dared.

"SSSSHH!" she hissed, looking around. Without taking her eyes off the kitchen door, she snatched another piece of pork and flipped it into the air. It arched high over my head. I leaped and caught it with a stunning mid-flight torso twist and, once again, dispensed with it hastily.

There were indeed perks to this new lifestyle.

"Mu 'yuk xa," she said, replacing the platter and closing the refrigerator door.

Bernice came in minutes later and escorted me out onto the courtyard, saying, "No dogs in the kitchen, understand?"

Mu 'yuk xa
(Tzotzil):
No more

21

Little did she know, dear reader, that I *did* understand.

After the family had eaten breakfast, Bernice and Hector each got ready for work. As Bernice had to leave earlier it was left to Hector to get Faith off to school. Plainly, she did not wish to go to school.

"I hate it," she answered when Hector asked why she didn't want to go.

Eventually he got her into the car despite her kicking and screaming, and off they went. Milagros got started on her housework — the dishes, the beds, the mopping, the laundry.

And I? I got down to dog's work. Marking my territory. Napping. Digging up the flower beds. Gnawing. Napping.

That afternoon, Faith rushed through the door, her eyes all red and swollen. She sank to her knees and hugged me and sobbed.

"Oh, Eddie," she said. "I hate it. I just hate it."

I pressed my muzzle up into her face and licked her cheek. It tasted salty.

"The kids at school hate me," she said. "The teacher hates me. I can't understand a thing anyone says and they can't understand me, either." She sniffled. "Diego keeps making fishy faces at me."

At that she buried her face into my neck and cried.

After a few minutes she pulled away and tried to

speak, but only big spit bubbles came out of her mouth. Horrid slimy goo oozed out of her nose. She wiped it all away with a swipe of her sleeve.

"Would you like to learn a new game?" she asked, snuffling.

The game was called Fetch. She threw a stick and I retrieved it. Quite simple, really. I caught on very quickly. Soon I was catching the stick in midair. We played until Faith was called into dinner, and then, after she'd eaten, I tugged her back outside. We played until it got too dark to see. All that night I lay awake thinking of fetching.

The next day when Faith came through the door after school, I greeted her, stick in mouth. Again, we played until dark, pausing only for dinner. I was obsessed. Dogged. Retrieval was all I could think about.

It got so that we played Fetch every afternoon and always on into the night. I was manic. I would wait for hours by the door with a stick in my mouth, drooling in anticipation.

Faith was a real trooper. She rarely denied me a toss. She'd stay up until she was fainting from fatigue, but still she threw. When finally she could go on no more, I would whine and whimper and paw. I slept with a stick in my mouth, just in case she should wake up and wish to play. I began having nightmares, too.

In one, Faith threw a stick high into the air and I

waited and waited for it to come down, but it never did. I just stood, poised and intent, staring skyward, waiting. I awoke in a sweat. In another, I chased down a thrown stick and just as I bent to scoop it up, it moved. Again I lunged at it, but again it danced out of reach. It began to taunt me, to tease me. Yes, it *spoke*. I chased it and chased it, but I never caught it, never retrieved.

Then, one day, as if from a dream, I saw Fetch for what it truly is: a monotonous, pointless waste of time. I remember laughing at how positively nutty I'd been.

Then she taught me Tug-of-war.

6
Faith Lost

Some afternoons, Faith's Spanish tutor, Socorro — everyone called her Coco — would come to the house to help Faith with her Spanish. Faith liked Coco. She liked her bright smile and glittering assortment of jewelry: woven bracelets, chain anklets, skull brooches, amber earrings. Faith liked one particular necklace very much. It was a small, shallow, silver box that had several long thin pieces of silver dangling from the bottom. The front of the box was hinged and had a clasp that you could open and close (if you had thumbs). Faith loved to open and close Coco's little silver box so much that Coco began wearing that particular necklace every time she came to visit, and she always put a little surprise inside for Faith.

There was only one thing about Coco that Faith

didn't like, and that was that she kept trying to teach Faith Spanish.

"It's a physical impossibility," Faith would say.

But Coco kept trying. Each time she came she had a surprise in her necklace and a new plan of attack.

Coco didn't teach Spanish with a textbook and a chalkboard and worksheets. No, no, nothing like that. She played games with Faith — card games, board games, running games, pretending games. She was very clever.

One day, she pretended to be Bernice and Faith pretended to be Hector and they pretended to have an argument. They talked about love and money — you know, grown-up stuff. The catch was that Coco spoke almost entirely in Spanish, and that Faith barely seemed to notice.

mercado
(Spanish): marketplace

☆

¡Tres pesos por cada papaya!
(Spanish): Three pesos for one papaya!

☆

Sí
(Spanish): Yes

On another day, Faith was a vendor in the *mercado* and Coco was a hungry customer with very little money. They both really hammed it up and, without realizing it, Faith began speaking in Spanish.

"¡Tres pesos por cada *papaya!"* Coco said.

Faith tried to look stern but ended up giggling and saying, *"Sí."*

Once, Coco helped Faith make what Coco called a family tree. Faith drew pictures of herself, her mother, Hector, Milagros, and me on colored paper. Then she cut the pictures out and glued them onto another piece of larger, stiffer paper and wrote the names of each of us under his or her picture. It was the first time I'd ever seen "Edison" spelled out, and I felt a little proud. It's a handsome word, very tall and straight on one end and very short and curved on the other.

Then Coco wrote a word under "Bernice."

"*Madre,*'" she read when she'd finished.

She wrote another word under "Hector."

"*Padrastro,*'" she said.

Beneath "Milagros" she wrote, and said, "*Amiga.*'"

Below my handsome name she wrote the words I'd so often heard before: "*Perro eléctrico.*'"

And under "Faith" she wrote a short little word.

"*Yo,*'" Faith read. "I know '*yo*' means 'I.' But how do I say 'Faith' in Spanish?"

"*¿Cómo?*" Coco asked, smiling.

"In Spanish?" Faith asked with a heavy sigh.

"*Sí, en español,*" Coco said.

Faith cleared her throat and said, "*¿Cómo se dice* 'Faith' *en español?*"

"*¡Bravo!*" Coco said, clapping her hands. "*¡Perfecto!*"

"*Gracias,*" Faith said, blushing.

"You can say 'Faith,'" Coco said. "In English or in Spanish, it's the same."

Faith seemed disappointed by this, and I think Coco sensed it.

madre
(Spanish):
mother

☆

padrastro
(Spanish):
stepfather

☆

amiga
(Spanish):
female friend

☆

yo
(Spanish): I

☆

¿Cómo?
(Spanish):
What?

☆

Sí, en español
(Spanish):
Yes, in Spanish

☆

¿Cómo se dice "Faith" en español?
(Spanish): How do you say "Faith" in Spanish?

"You can also say '*Fe*,'" she told Faith. "*Fe* is Spanish for 'faith,' like when you believe in something."

Faith smiled.

"*Fe*," she said. "Swell!"

It was on one of the afternoons that Coco came by that the roof fell in.

Bernice had gone to pick up Faith from school and Coco had been waiting a long time for them to return. She kept checking her watch and walking up and down. Milagros assured her, in Spanish, that they'd be home any minute. But on and on we waited.

Finally, Coco said she had to leave. She gave Milagros a hug and said, "*No te preocupes, mi hija.*" Then she got her coat, rubbed my head, and left.

The sun was nearly down and I just couldn't sit and wait any longer. I barked and barked and howled by the front gate until Milagros finally opened it, and then out into the streets of San Cristóbal de las Casas I ran, back out into those familiar, unfriendly streets to find the one who had rescued me from them.

7
Electric Shoes

I raced through the narrow cobblestone paths of El
Cerrillo, through the feet of the tourists shopping
for handicrafts in the plaza of Santo Domingo, past
the cathedral and the *zócalo* and the little hill (El Cerrito) in the center of town with the little church on
top. The sky was darkening and the air was chilling
and my heart was pounding.

Old street dog chums called out as I passed but I
did not acknowledge them. I had far to go and no
time to lose. I crossed streets without looking. I
passed food scraps without slowing. I was ignoring
instincts I'd spent my whole life developing. All I
could think about was finding Faith. Nothing else
mattered.

When I finally crossed the small bridge that spans
the stream around Faith's school, I found Bernice's

zócalo
(Spanish):
town square

funny little red car in the parking lot. Parked next to it was a police car, with flashing red and white lights.

I hurried up the path to the school, which was a cluster of round adobe huts. The lights were on in one of them. I saw Bernice through the window talking to several other people, including a police officer. She looked quite beside herself and was waving her arms about as if she was some great bird. I sized up the situation quickly: Faith was missing.

I put my nose to work and within a few minutes I was able to pick up my master's scent. It led me down a path out behind the school and through the trees. The sun had set completely now. There were no lights, except the stars above. I was at the mercy of my snout.

Her scent led me past the spot by the stream where I'd first seen her. I forded the stream and picked her scent up again on the other side. Brave girl! Brave, foolish (and probably soaking wet) Faith!

I crossed a pasture where horses stood sleeping and, in the darkness, trod in their droppings several times. I got snagged in thistle bushes. I got caught on barbed wire. But I did not lose Faith's scent.

panteón
(Spanish): graveyard; cemetery

It led me into the *panteón*.

I slipped through a hole in the fence and followed my nose past wooden crosses decorated with plastic flowers. These were the grave markings of the people of San Cristóbal de las Casas who had died with little or no money. I climbed the hill toward the more spectacular mausoleums and shrines, in which were laid the city's richer dead folk. Many of the sites were still decorated from the Days of the Dead.

On those days — the first two days of November — the people of Mexico visit the graves of their dear departed and stay throughout the night. They bring with them the favorite foods and belongings of their loved ones to lure them from the beyond. They decorate the graves with candles and bouquets of bright orange marigolds. They sing the dead's favorite songs and the children wear masks and play with toy skeletons and eat candied skulls. The cemetery is filled with light and song and laughter. It's a party for the dead.

You see, in Mexico the dead are not feared — they are welcomed. And graveyards are lively places.

But I knew Faith was not from Mexico, and I'd heard that, to North Americans, cemeteries are spooky places. So I speeded up my search.

I tracked her scent all around the *panteón,* until I found I was covering the same ground — going around in circles. Obviously, she'd gotten lost. On the outside chance that she was nearby, I howled.

I heard back only my echo.

Fog settled in, wrapping the dimly lit *panteón* in an eerie cloak of mist. The air temperature dropped. I felt the dampness in my bones. I wondered if Faith had worn her jacket.

I howled again. Again, just my echo.

I continued the search. Round and round the gravestones I went. It seemed useless, but what else could I do? I traced and retraced my steps.

Finally, exhausted, I crawled up onto a tall sky-blue crypt to think.

The hill that the *panteón* sits atop lies between the school and town. From my vantage point, I looked down on the city nestled in the valley below, all lit up with streetlights and the headlights of cars.

The sun had set and a crescent moon glimmered behind the wispy fog. I could hear roosters crowing and dogs howling, and so, once again, I howled. I howled from deep down inside of me — from my belly.

When you're blue, there's nothing quite like howling at the moon.

I don't know how long I'd been howling when I noticed a tiny red flash of light below, down in the cow pastures that separate the *panteón* from town. Then I saw another one. Each of the flashes lasted less than a second. After the second, there was a third, then a fourth. There was a rhythm to their appearance. After a moment or two I remember deciding that there were just two lights and that they were taking turns flashing: they were alternating. One, two. One, two. One, two. It wasn't an automobile's taillights — they wouldn't alternate. They would glow together. It looked to me as if these tiny red lights were *walking*.

And that's when I remembered Faith's *zapatos eléctricos* — her electric shoes! The ones that blinked red with each and every step! (They were — and still are — commonly worn by children from the United States.)

zapatos eléctricos
(Spanish):
electric shoes

I jumped from the crypt and darted as quickly as I could down the hill, through the gates of the *panteón,* and along the dirt road toward town and Faith's blinking feet.

When I was within earshot, I began to bark. The red lights went out and I lost where she was. I guessed that she had stopped. I continued running in the same direction I'd been, and just hoped I'd bump into her.

And then the red lights began blinking again, only much more rapidly than they had before. She was running! Running away!

I barked louder but the lights only blinked faster.

"Go away!" Faith yelled. "Go away, devil dog! *¡Afuera! ¡Afuera!*"

I found — to my relief — that I run much faster than Faith and was able to gain on her fairly easily. I ran past her and headed her off. She skidded to a stop and stood heaving and sobbing and shaking (she *was* soaking wet and she *didn't* have her jacket on).

"Eh-Eh-Eddie?" she said.

I barked.

She rushed me and I jumped up and licked her salty face.

"Oh, Eddie!" she said, giggling. "Good boy! Good boy!"

8
Faith's Bright Idea

As we walked back to her school, Faith told me why she had run away. In a word: Diego. He had filled her lunch box with *orugas quemadores*. She'd lost control and banged him over the head with it. The orugas had spilled out onto Diego's face and neck and arms. (Faith smiled as she remembered that part.) Her *maestra* entered the room just at that moment, and seeing Diego shrieking and flailing about, she rushed to help him. The children were all trying to explain to the maestra what had happened, and, naturally, they spoke in Spanish. Faith was so embarrassed and flustered and scared that she just bolted out the door and ran off. *Pobrecita*.

She told me that when she was wandering lost in the *panteón* she had heard the howling of some terrible beast. She'd figured it was a devil dog risen from the grave to devour her.

orugas quemadores
(Spanish): furry black caterpillars that sting when touched

☆

maestra
(Spanish): female teacher

☆

pobrecita
(Spanish): poor thing (female)

It had probably been me.

We climbed the hill in silence, passed back through the *panteón,* and then walked across the horse pasture.

"I want to go home," she said to me as we crossed back over the bridge to her school. "All the way home."

I wasn't sure then exactly what she meant by that.

When Bernice saw Faith step sheepishly into the room, she seemed shocked, then puzzled, then outraged, but all the time completely speechless. Finally, she flung herself at her daughter, first hugging her, then shaking her, then madly kissing her, then scolding her, then hugging her again. It was quite disorienting, I can tell you. In the end, she dragged poor dizzy Faith out to the funny little red car and strapped her in. I piled into the backseat. So far, Bernice hadn't seemed even to notice me. She was very busy telling Faith in great detail just how terrified and worried she'd been. Faith just stared at her own feet.

Now, despite all the commotion and excitement, I really must admit that all I could think about was that, for the first time, I was about to go for a ride in an automobile. For once, I was to be in the belly of the beast rather than scurrying out of its way.

Bernice threw the car into gear and sped down the dirt road from the school to the highway. I instinctively put my head out the window and felt the dusty wind blowing in my face.

"Edison!" Bernice yelled. "Edison!"

I pulled my head in.

"Keep your head inside the car," she barked.

She had Faith roll up my window so that all I could do was press my snout up against the glass.

Neither Bernice nor Faith spoke as we drove toward town. Bernice just scowled and grumbled. Faith continued to study her shoes.

On Avenida Insurgentes, I saw Groorf and Browl, and when they spotted me they chased the car for several blocks. I felt smug and spoiled, but also a little nauseous.

As we began our climb up El Cerrillo, Faith finally spoke.

"I want to go home," she said.

"We *are* going home," Bernice said.

"No," Faith said. "I want to go *home* home."

"*Home* home?" Bernice asked.

They both sat quietly for a moment, then Bernice asked, "Do you mean San Francisco?"

Faith nodded.

"Well, I'm sorry to burst your bubble, sweetheart," Bernice said, "but we're staying right here."

"No, I'm going home," Faith said.

"Oh, you *are*, are you? How?"

"I don't know," Faith said miserably.

"Uh-huh," Bernice said.

"I'll fly home," Faith said.

"And who's going to pay for your plane ticket?" Bernice asked. "Certainly not me."

Faith frowned.

"I'll take the bus," she said. "I have money in my doggie bank."

"Not nearly enough," Bernice said with a snort.

Faith crossed her arms and thought some more.

"I'll swim!" she said.

Bernice looked at her with one eyebrow cocked and shook her head slowly.

"You're an odd little girl," she said.

"I'm a good swimmer," Faith said.

"What about sharks?" her mother asked.

Faith brought her crossed arms up under her chin and grunted. She sounded defeated.

"You better just get used to it, missy," Bernice said. "Like it or not, we're staying right here. You included. I suggest that —"

"I'll build a rocket ship!" Faith said, rising up as high in her seat as her seat belt would allow.

"A *what?!*" Bernice said.

"A rocket ship!" Faith said. "I'll build a rocket ship and fly back to San Francisco!"

Bernice pulled the car over and stopped. We were home. She turned and looked seriously at Faith.

"Why, Faith?" she asked. "Why do you want to go back so much?"

"Because I hate it here!" Faith said wildly. "I hate Mexico and I hate Mexicans!"

I didn't like that.

"Faith!" Bernice said, bringing her fingers to her mouth. "What a terrible thing to say! Hector's Mexican, you know!"

So am I, I remember thinking.

"You know what I mean," Faith said, sinking down in her seat.

"Is that why you ran away from school today?" Bernice asked.

"I'm going to build a rocket ship and I'm going to fly home," Faith said defiantly. "And Eddie's going with me! Huh, Eddie?"

Me? I thought. But I'm Mexican.

9
The *Peahen*

There's a man in the *mercado,* Señor Latas, who makes all sorts of things out of tin cans. Candleholders, watering cans, planters, and those little grills the *indígenas* use to roast corn. Faith had always loved Señor Latas's things, and so she decided to ask him to build her a rocket ship. The only problem was that she didn't know the words.

She asked Coco, "*¿Cómo se dice* 'I want you to build me a rocket out of tin, please'?"

Coco shortened it for her.

"*Dices, 'Quiero un cohete, por favor.'*"

"Key-eddo oon ko-ate-tay, por fa-vore," Faith repeated. "Right?"

"*Perfecto,*" Coco said.

Faith practiced all evening in front of the mirror until she had it down pat. The next morning, she took me with her to the *mercado.*

¿Cómo se dice . . . ?
(Spanish): How do you say . . . ?

☆

Dices, "Quiero un cohete, por favor"
(Spanish): Say "I want a rocket, please"

As we wove through the crowds I saw Yip, one of my old pals from my street days.

"Who's the little girl?" he asked me in Bowwow. "And what's with the rope?"

I explained as best I could about my leash and that the little girl at the other end of it was my new master, and that she was completely crazy.

"Ah, too bad," he said. "You're looking well-fed, though, Grumph."

"Can't complain, can't complain," I said.

"So, I hear you're inside these days," Yip said.

"Yeah," I said.

"Well, how do you like it?"

"It has its good points," I said.

"They got you up on a roof?"

"No," I said. It's common practice in San Cristóbal de las Casas to keep dogs chained up in pens on rooftops.

"How's Mark been?" I asked.

"Not so well," Yip said. "Parvovirus. Bad. Real bad."

"Sorry to hear that," I said. "Mark's a good dog."

"Yup," said Yip.

"Come on, Eddie," Faith said and gave a tug on the lead.

"Master beckons," Yip said with a smirk.

"Say hey to everyone," I said.

"Will do," Yip said. "Later."

compadres
*(Spanish): pals;
chums*

Buenos días
*(Spanish): Good
morning*

**Quieres un
¿qué?**
*(Spanish): You
want what?*

**No entiendo,
señorita**
*(Spanish): I
don't under-
stand, miss*

He disappeared into the crowd and a sulky sadness sank in on me. I missed my *compadres*.

We reached Señor Latas's booth, and before he could even say *"Buenos días,"* Faith blurted:

"Key-eddo oon ko-ate-tay, por fa-vore!"

"Quieres un ¿qué?" he said.

Faith didn't understand, so she just repeated her question, only more loudly and more slowly. Señor Latas just scratched his head and said, *"No entiendo, señorita."*

Faith was on the verge of tears.

"Oh!" she said, pumping her fists and stomping her feet. "I *hate* Mexico!"

Now remember, dear reader, she was frustrated and confused. She also didn't know that I could understand her. Perhaps she didn't even think of me as Mexican. I don't think she meant it as an insult. I doubt that she even realized it *was* an insult. But it was, and it hurt.

"May I be of any assistance?" said a voice from behind us.

We turned to find an elderly woman wearing a sombrero. Her skin was pale but reddened from the sun, and her hair under her hat was white.

"What?" Faith said.

"Now, now, darling," the woman said. "What seems to be the trouble, hmmm?"

I could tell by the woman's accent that she was

from England, though I don't know where England is. I just know accents. Hers was British.

"Now it's all right, dear," she said. "Perhaps I could help. My Spanish is atrocious, but they do seem to understand me well enough."

Faith just stared.

"Do you want to buy something from this gentleman?" the woman asked.

Faith nodded.

The woman waited patiently for Faith to tell her more. It was clear that the woman was a worldly sort who did not wish to become engaged in a guessing game.

"I want a rocket ship," Faith said at last.

"Ah, a rocket ship," the woman said. "Shall I ask if he has one about someplace?"

"He doesn't have one," Faith said. "I want him to *make* one for me."

"Can he?" the woman said.

"I don't know," Faith said. "Hector told me he can make anything out of tin cans."

"Hector?" the woman asked, then shook her head. "Never mind that. Yes, well, he certainly does have plenty of things made out of tin. I'll just inquire, shall I?"

She turned to Señor Latas and spoke in passable Spanish.

Faith, naturally, couldn't understand, though I think she did understand Señor Latas's answer.

"No," he said.

"Pleeeeeeze," Faith said.

Señor Latas looked down into Faith's eyes. They were damp and heartbreaking. He spoke again to the woman, who turned to Faith and said, "He says he just might be able to manage it."

"Yay!" Faith said, startling Señor Latas.

"He wants to know what it's to look like," the woman said.

Eagerly, Faith dug into her pocket and pulled out a crumpled piece of paper and handed it to the woman.

"Oh, how marvelous!" the woman said when she had uncrumpled it. "It looks like a peacock."

The woman showed it to Señor Latas. He examined it with a serious expression, then spoke to the woman again.

"How large is it to be?" she asked Faith.

Faith looked around and found one of Señor Latas's planters. She upended it, and climbed on top. Then she reached her hand as high over her head as she could. This meant getting up on her tiptoes.

"Oh my!" the woman said.

Señor Latas slapped his cheek with his palm.

"¡Ay caramba!" he said.

With the woman's help, Señor Latas explained to

No
(Spanish): No

¡Ay caramba!
(Spanish): Oh, my goodness!

Faith how long it would take to build the rocket and how much it would cost, and Faith just kept saying "Okay."

She went back each day and asked *"¿Ya?"* and Señor Latas always said *"No,"* until finally one morning he said *"¡Sí!"*

Faith broke her doggie bank and gave the money to Señor Latas, and he closed up shop and helped her carry the rocket home. Bernice was in the courtyard replanting some fuchsias I'd dug up. She dropped her watering can.

"Wha—?" she said.

"Mama, this is Señor Latas," Faith said.

"Buenos días, señora," Señor Latas said.

Bernice gave him a little nod. She was staring at the rocket with her mouth open.

"Over here, Señor," Faith said, pointing.

They carried the ship past Bernice to an open space on the patio and set it down with a clank.

"Gracias," Faith said.

"De nada," Señor Latas said.

Then Señor Latas tipped his hat to Bernice, said, *"Adiós, señora,"* and left.

Bernice walked around and around the rocket ship.

"Well?" Faith said.

"It's a rocket," Bernice said.

"It's *my* rocket," Faith said.

"It looks like a giant silver peacock," Bernice said.

¿Ya?
(Spanish):
Ready yet?

señora
(Spanish):
ma'am; title
for a married
woman

De nada
(Spanish):
You're welcome

☆

Adiós
(Spanish):
Good-bye

It did. It was a stout column of tin, with two tin fins attached to its sides. The fins were cut into a wavelike design so that they looked somewhat like flames, or the tail feathers of a peacock. There was one round window cut into the body and there was a cone on top, the tip of which drooped over to one side like the tip of a jester's cap. It looked a bit like a beak.

"It's not a *boy* rocket, Mama," Faith said. "A peacock's a boy bird." She thought a minute and then asked, "What's a girl peacock called?"

Bernice, still a little stunned, stammered, "What? What, Faith?"

"A girl peacock. What do you call a girl peacock?"

"Uh . . . a peahen, I think," Bernice said. "Yes, a peahen. But they don't have the plumage that a —"

"A peahen," Faith mumbled, then brightened. "That's it! I'll call her the *Peahen*!"

10
The Cockroach
Is Me

Next came the business of getting the *Peahen* to fly.

"It all has to do with gravity," Faith told me a number of times. Other times she just fiddled with her lower lip and muttered, "Gravity, gravity, gravity."

With aluminum foil and a cardboard toilet-paper tube, she built a model rocket and filled it with lard and a teaspoon of chile pepper oil. Then, with a match she'd tied to a long stick, she lit the fuse. I cowered over in the corner, under a patio chair, with my paws over my eyes. To my great horror, the little rocket went up a meter or two, but then, fortunately, burst into flames and nosedived into Bernice's compost heap.

Instinctively I rushed from my hiding place and fetched the charred remains.

Old habits die hard.

For the next model Faith replaced the pepper oil with minced poblano chiles and put astronauts in the model's cone. There was a caterpillar, representing Faith, and a cockroach, representing me. I did not approve of the casting.

"Ten . . . nine . . . eight . . . seven . . . six . . . five . . ." Faith said. "Four . . . three . . . two . . . one . . . ignition . . . blast off!"

She touched the match to the fuse. With a fizzle and a flare the little ship lifted off the patio, struggling with all its might against the forces of nature.

"Go, little *Peahen,*" Faith said softly, her hands clasped tightly together.

But at around four meters up or so, the little *Peahen* began to zigzag. It coughed and did a fancy aerial loop before plunging back earthward. Centimeters before impact it belched out a plume of black smoke and, as if suddenly determined to make one more go of it, changed course. It streamed along close to the ground directly at yours truly, where I had resumed my cowardly position under the patio chair.

I was so startled I couldn't move.

"Yowr-rr-rr!" I said as it crashed into me.

I jumped up and my head stuck through the rubber straps of the chair's seat. Panicked, I fled, dragging the chair with me.

Yowr-rr-rr!
(Bowwow):
Yee-ouch!

48

Faith ran over to me. Out of concern for my well-being? Not exactly.

"Is it hurt?" she asked as she disentangled the rocket from my fur. "Did they survive?"

Apparently, my welfare came third, after the model's and the insect astronauts'.

She popped off the cone and peered in. Her nose wrinkled. She looked at me and forced a smile.

"Casualties," she said with a shrug.

We buried the brave little astronauts at the base of a peach tree.

The problem, she told me, was in the combustion. She spoke of thrust and oxidizers and escape velocities, but I didn't understand any of it and wondered whether she did. She tried a variety of different peppers and she replaced the lard first with molasses, then with refried beans, then polenta. Nothing worked.

Within days, we'd begun a small *panteón* under that peach tree.

But Faith did not give up.

She no longer sang me songs. She no longer read me stories. She no longer gave me baths (well, okay, I didn't mind that). At night, she'd sit at her desk reading books about rockets, scribbling down notes, and muttering. In the afternoons, after school, she'd test out her ideas — launching model after model, each one going a little higher than the last, but each one inevitably sputtering and crashing to earth.

I admired her persistence. But I missed her.

There is a *dicho* in Mexico that goes: *"El que quiera azul celeste, que le cueste."*

Gradually, I began to think that her little scheme was simply not going to work. I remember how smug I became. I even stopped watching the launches. I was certain they would fall. I'd worried over nothing, I told myself. Soon, I thought, she'd realize that neither Mexico nor Mexicans meant her any harm and that, with perseverance, she'd find that she could adjust — maybe even flourish — in San Cristóbal de las Casas. Then she'd give up this crazy notion of building a rocket ship and settle down into her new life.

It was with this false sense of security that I waltzed into the kitchen for supper that fateful evening.

11
Pork

I'd been drawn to the kitchen by a mesmerizing aroma that had drifted out to the courtyard where I was busy doing absolutely nothing. I knew the smell like I knew the back of my paw.

Carnitas.

I trotted casually into the kitchen as if I'd done so for some other reason. Bernice was there and, to show her that I was a well-behaved, obedient house dog, I didn't jump up on her and try to bite her hand.

For a dog, that requires fierce self-discipline.

Milagros had removed the sizzling *carnitas* from the oven and was drizzling *manteca* over the golden slab of meat. If you've never seen this done, you've missed something truly dazzling.

Without my knowledge, my tongue spilled out of my mouth.

manteca
(Spanish): fat

"*¡Afuera!*" Bernice yelled.

I pulled my tongue in with a slurp.

"*¡Afuera!*" she repeated.

I decided to play along and bank on Faith or Milagros coming through with the goods once again. Giving Bernice my most doleful expression, I slunk out, curled up on the mat just outside the door, and settled for inhaling the glorious fragrance of the *manteca,* unaware as I was then of its varied uses.

Faith did not think to bring me any *carnitas* that night — she was too preoccupied with her precious rocket ship — so the next morning I begged for scraps from Milagros. She took the platter from the fridge and dug out a large, luscious chunk for me, which was covered in solid white pig fat. Yum.

Suddenly, footsteps from behind caused us both to freeze.

"Oh, Milagros," a voice said.

Whew. Just Faith.

I ate the forbidden morsel and Milagros hurriedly replaced the platter.

"Wait," Faith said just as Milagros was beginning to close the refrigerator door.

Faith moved forward and took the platter from the

shelf. She plunged a finger deep into the cold *man-teca.*

"Eureka!" she said.

I didn't know that word then, dear reader, but I do now.

That afternoon, after school, model #13 took its maiden voyage. It was filled with diced jalapeño peppers and — you guessed it — pig fat. Once again, it was piloted by a caterpillar and a cockroach. For some reason — call it a hunch, call it a premonition of doom — I remember deciding to hang around for this launch. I tipped the patio chair over on its side and peered through the slats.

"Ten . . . nine . . . eight . . . seven . . . six . . . five . . ." Faith said, lying on her belly, match in hand. "Four . . . three . . . two . . . one . . . ignition . . . blast off!"

She lit the fuse and when the flame reached the rocket, there was a fizzling sound. The little ship trembled a bit, then a bit harder, until it nearly fell over. Then, in a flash, it shot into the air. Within seconds, it was completely out of sight!

"Hooo!" Faith said as she slowly rose to her feet, her hand shading her eyes from the sun as she stared up into the sky. She looked over at me and grinned.

"Did you see that, Eddie?"

I'd seen it.

Her grin swelled into a great big broad smile. She danced a little jig, and began to sing:

"Uh rum sum sum
"Uh rum sum sum
"Gooey gooey gooey gooey rum sum sum . . ."

12
Blast Off

We sat inside the *Peahen* on pine chairs that Faith had varnished bright red. The chairs sat atop the fuel tank — a large tin container made to Faith's specifications by Señor Latas, and filled with the pig fat that Faith had purchased from the *mercado*'s meat market. The smell of it was maddening. And to think it would all be burned away! *¡Qué lástima!*

Faith ran through her systems check.

"*Chicles,*" she said.

She pulled a pack of chewing gum out of her shirt pocket.

"Check," she said, and checked it off her list.

"Map," she said.

She looked under her seat.

"Check," she said, and checked it off.

She ran through the list (purified water, chocolate,

¡Qué lástima!
(Spanish): What a shame!

☆

Chicles
(Spanish): chewing gum

pillows, kibbles, matches, jalapeños, water wings, *Higglety Pigglety Pop!,* and, of course, *manteca*).

"T minus one minute," she said.

She had dropped some minced jalapeños into the fuel tank a few minutes before systems check, and had closed the little hinged door that sealed it. A long fuse came out of a hole in the little door. The length of the fuse coiled around our chairs. Faith held the other end of it in her hand.

"T minus thirty seconds," she said.

I remember realizing then that, even if I had had a say in the matter — which I hadn't — I probably would have chosen to go with her. I was surprised by this realization. As you know, dear reader, I had been against her harebrained scheme from the get-go. Yet it occurred to me then, for the first time, that I'd go anywhere, do anything, for her, including flying away from all that I had ever known in a rocket ship. It must have been the dog in me. We're true blue. Even electric ones.

"Countdown," Faith said. "Ten . . . nine . . . eight . . ."

I strained to look out the small circular window on Faith's side. I could see peaches in the trees — peach trees fertilized by dead cockroaches, cockroaches that had stood in for me.

"Three . . . two . . . one . . . ignition . . . blast off!"

She lit the fuse, and the flame ran along it down to the floor beside me and then around my chair. Neither of us breathed as we watched the fire creep nearer and nearer the fuel. Five seconds or more passed before it reached the hole in the little door and disappeared into the tank.

I vaguely remember hearing something hiss and then there was a tremendous roar.

Imagine, dear reader, that an enormous giant has grasped your head with his very large hands, and then commences to shake it with every ounce of strength that he can muster. Got that? Okay. Now, he lifts you off the ground by your head, all the while continuing to shake and twist it, and slams your body repeatedly to the ground. Are you imagining this, dear reader? The shaking, the lifting, the pounding? Okay then, now, now, this evil creature sets into hollering. Remember that he is very very large with a very very large mouth and very very large lungs. He doesn't yell anything in particular. Just "Aaargh!" or something. Can you hear him? Can you imagine the violent twisting, the jerking, the hullabaloo?

If you have a good imagination, you can probably sense just how discombobulating an experience this would surely be.

Do your best.

For this is similar, though surely not equal, to the

experience of blasting off in Faith's confounded little death craft.

My deepest, most heartfelt sympathies go out to those innocent little cockroaches and caterpillars.

It seemed an eternity that I was shaken so. But it was probably more along the line of five minutes. In that time I'd forgotten all about Faith and the pig fat and the laws of nature. It was true pandemonium. I vaguely remember noticing Faith bounce past me a couple of times, but then again, everything bounced past me a couple of times: kibbles, chocolate bars, *Higglety Pigglety Pop!* It was very much like being a bean in a maraca, I suspect.

But after those five minutes, the noise and vibration died down and all the objects came to rest, including Faith and myself. Faith was crumpled up, face down, in the corner. Her green gum had apparently popped out of her mouth and gotten stuck in her orange hair. (Color-blind indeed!)

"Eddie," she said. "You all right?"

I whined.

She righted herself and crawled back up into her chair. I inched my way over to her and wrapped myself around her feet. She reached down and gave me a little scratch behind the collar.

For the moment, the ship was fairly still. I could hear the groaning of rivets and the flapping of sheets of tin being bowed by the rushing air, and I could hear the roar of the engine, though it sounded quieter than before.

"Come see," Faith said, looking out the window. "We're flying."

Now, I knew that people sometimes rode in airplanes and I'd often seen helicopters over San Cristóbal de las Casas, which, I knew, carried people. I'd even heard that sometimes people brought their pets along with them in little cages on flights.

But I had never flown, and I discovered that, despite how scared I was, I eagerly wished to see.

I climbed up onto Faith's lap.

Out the window I saw the pointy green mountaintops of Chiapas that I'd seen my entire life, only now, for the first time, from above. San Cristóbal de las Casas was far below and beyond. I recognized its red-tiled rooftops and its little churches on its little hilltops. In the distance I could seen cornfields and the squiggly Río Amarillo cutting through them.

It was lovely.

"It's so pretty," Faith said.

She smiled and a tear streamed down her cheek.

"*Adiós,* Mama," she said, tearfully. "*Adiós,* Hector and Milagros and Coco and Señor Latas. *Adiós,* San Cristóbal de las Casas!"

13
The Sky, the Sea, and the Storm

Faith dug the map out from under the debris and unfolded it.

"We're around here somewhere," she said, pointing to a hooked shape on the map.

"The Gulf of Mexico is north of us," she said. "The Caribbean is to the east and the Pacific Ocean is to the west and south."

(If you didn't get out an atlas or encyclopedia before when I suggested it, now might be a good time. Don't you think?)

Below, the mountains were giving way to treeless desert.

"I think that's Tuxtla-Gutiérrez," Faith said.

Out the window, I could see a city creeping toward us (or rather I could see that we were creeping toward a city). It looked much bigger than San Cristóbal de las Casas. Some of the buildings were as tall as El Cerrito.

The *Peahen* had turned somehow. We were traveling at a much slighter incline upward, and it seemed to be decreasing all the time. In fact, we were very close to riding along parallel to the earth. To compensate for this, Faith and I had to put our chairs on the wall.

"Soon we'll be able to see Popo," Faith said. "The volcano."

We passed over lakes and mountains and fields — places the likes of which I'd never seen, and probably never would have seen if it hadn't been for this willful child. It was thrilling. My fears soon disappeared and I found myself hoping that it would take us a very long time to reach San Francisco, California.

Vapors were rising up out of the mouth of Popo as we passed over it. *C'est magnifique!*

After Popo, we passed over Mexico City, the most populated city in the world, according to Faith. Then came Guadalajara, another sprawling city, and then we flew out over the sea.

I'd never seen an ocean before, living all my life, as I had, high up in the landlocked Chiapas highlands. Initially, I imagined it to be an expanse of fields of blue corn, or blue grass, or blue trees. It looked to me to be moving. The farther we got out over it, the

C'est magnifique!
(French): It's magnificent!

61

more I could see that it was truly immense. It went out beyond my sight in all directions. It was the biggest thing, next to the sky, that I'd ever seen.

"We're nearing Cabo San Lucas," Faith said, and, sure enough, far off in the distance, I could see land again.

"It's on the very tip of Baja California," she told me and pointed to a long, fingerlike shape on the map.

"That's the Pacific on the left, and on the right's the Gulf of California."

California? I remember thinking. Already?

As if she could read my mind she added, "Not the *American* California. The *Mexican* California."

Oh, I thought. I didn't know there were two.

We soared over Baja California Sur, past Bahía de la Paz (the Bay of Peace), over Isla Santa Margarita and Isla Santa Magdalena (which are islands), over the Sierra Vizcaino mountains, past Bahía Tortugas (Turtle Bay), and over Isla La Navidad (Christmas Island).

It was just after Christmas Island that the sky began to darken and our blissful joyride took a turn for the worse. Funny how suddenly weather changes. You just never know what's waiting to happen next, do you?

"Uh-oh," Faith said.

The sound of the wind grew harsher and the creaking of the *Peahen*'s metal grew creakier. Soon the sky and the sea turned gray and ominous. In the distance we could see bolts of lightning streaking from cloud to cloud and from cloud to sea. The sky looked as if it were tumbling down into the ocean.

"Rain," Faith said.

Right she was. Within seconds we were in it. Out the window you could see nothing but sheets of rain. The *Peahen* heaved and spun and lurched. Frustrated, Faith tossed the map away.

And my fear returned.

14
The Bone

Rain spells trouble for dogs. It washes away scents. Dogs live by their noses and when nothing smells, dogs get lost.

Evidently, the same thing happened to Faith. Like a dog in the rain, she got lost. Unfortunately, she was the pilot.

We flew blindly into the storm, which became fiercer and fiercer. I crawled under my chair and sniveled. Sniveling has a calming effect. Faith sat beside me on the floor, massaging my shoulders, kissing me on the snout, saying "It's all right, buddy. It's all right." But after a while she began to snivel, too, and I licked away her tears. Outside, thunderclaps clapped and lightning lit up the darkened clouds.

Faith began to sing "Rum Sum Sum," in a soft voice, with a scared face.

The rain and the wind pressed our little spacecraft down, down, downward. Faith and I scratched our way to the window and clutched its rim, hoping to catch a glimpse of anything as we fell. All we could see out the window was a thin mist, grayness, and swirling rain, punctuated by flashes of light.

"Things don't look good," Faith said.

I wanted to tell her not to worry, but even if I could have spoken her language, I don't think I could have said that.

Down we went. I could feel it in my stomach.

Lightning flashed and I saw the white crests of waves below, closer than I'd have liked. A second flash and we were closer still.

"Prepare for a splash landing," Faith said.

I stayed glued to the window while she rushed about, clearly not knowing what to do.

The sky lit up once more and below us, for a split second, I saw land! A small island!

The shape of it seemed familiar, comforting, inviting.

It was bone-shaped.

"Time to bail!" Faith screamed.

I didn't like this idea. Not at all.

But Faith had already opened the hatch and was prepared to jump. She grabbed me by the collar and dragged me to her.

"*Grar-ark!*" I said.

Grar-ark!
(Bowwow):
No way!

65

Out the hatch I could see the ocean's surface below, surging past us, and I wondered what monstrous beasts lurked beneath it. Monstrous beasts with great, horrible, jagged teeth.

In seconds the ship would splash down. Faith held me under her left arm and, with her right, braced herself against the ship. She took a deep breath and closed her eyes.

"One . . . two . . . three . . . Geronimo!"

She pushed off and we dropped like stones, through the driving rain, down, down, down into the shark-infested Pacific.

I'd never had the occasion to learn to swim, a fact that I regretted the moment I hit the freezing, churning waters of the ocean. The force of the fall drove me deep down under the waves, deeper than I felt comfortable going. I paddled vigorously to halt my descent and, eventually, I stopped sinking and began to climb.

I kept my eyes open but could see nothing except dark blueness all around. No sharks, no beasts, no Faith. Finally, I reached the surface and soon had devised a version of dog-paddling that enabled me to keep afloat reasonably well.

"Eddie!" I heard Faith yell.

I turned and saw her riding a tall wave above me. The swell lifted me up to her.

"Oh, Eddie," she said as she snagged me.

The wave crested, then crashed. Down we went again, only this time we managed to hold onto each other.

When we resurfaced I remembered the island I'd seen — the bone-shaped one — and began madly paddling in the direction I believed it to be (the middle of the ocean is a very disorienting place). Faith must have sensed my conviction, for she swam right along with me without saying a word.

"Look!" Faith said, after we'd paddled awhile.

I'd already spotted it. The skies had begun to clear and the treetops of the island could be seen plainly over the waves. By the time the island was in full view, the sky and the sea were blue once more. Large white birds circled overhead and visions of sharks nibbling at my paws spurred me to swim onward.

The island was very green with many tall trees. As we drew closer I could see the coastline was sandy beach. (I recognized this from snapshots Faith had shown me of San Francisco, California.) In my estimation, we were at one of the ends of the bone, not at the shaft.

The water became clearer as we neared the beach. Faith was able to stand before I was, so she scooped me up in her arms, laughed, and carried me the rest of the way.

"Good dog," she said, out of breath.

15
The Electric Dogs

The next thing I remember was being awakened the next morning on the beach by the licking and sniffing of electric dogs.

There were four of them. I knew they were electric dogs because they had floppy ears and furrowed brows and because they understood me when I spoke Bowwow.

"Ruff!" I said.

"Ruff, boo-foo!" one of them barked.

The commotion woke Faith.

"Where are we?" Faith asked.

"Where are we?" I asked the dogs in Bowwow.

"Who are you?" one of the dogs asked me. He was thin and dark brown and was definitely the leader. Every pack has one. I later learned his name was Bark.

"Oh, I remember," Faith said.

Ruff!
(Bowwow):
Hey!

☆

Ruff, boo-foo!
(Bowwow):
Hey, yourself!

"I'm Grumph," I said to Bark, "and this is my master."

"We jumped out of the *Peahen* and swam to shore," Faith said to herself. "I guess we must have slept here on the beach last night. Funny. I don't remember falling asleep."

When she spoke the dogs seemed hypnotized.

"Why, hello poochy woochy poos," Faith said, apparently just noticing them.

They all took a synchronized step backward.

"I'm not going to hurt you," she said, crouching. "Come on, come on, yes."

"What does she want?" Bark asked.

"To be friends, I guess," I said.

"What's a master?" said another dog, Fruff, a tan female with large black spots.

"Aren't there masters on this island?" I asked.

Faith kept creeping closer to the dogs. They kept creeping away.

"What's a master?" Fruff repeated.

"She takes care of me," I said. "Masters are people who take care of dogs."

"People?" the third dog, Woo-Woof, asked. He was gray and probably about a year old.

"There aren't any people here?" I asked.

"There's nothing like *that* here," Fruff said. "Is she some sort of bird?"

"She doesn't have feathers," Bark said sternly.

"Or a tail," the last dog said. Her name was Ro-Ro and she was charcoal-black.

"Yeah," Fruff said.

"Can you understand the noises she makes?" Bark asked.

"Yes," I said.

"Can she understand us?" Woo-Woof said, alarmed.

"No," I said.

"Is she safe?" Fruff asked.

"Not really," I said.

Ro-Ro approached Faith first, cautiously, her head hung low. Bark followed closely behind.

"That's a coo-coo widdle pupper-wupper," my master said to Ro-Ro, and scratched between her ears.

Moments later, Faith had an armful of hounds. They grew so enthusiastic that they knocked her to the ground. She didn't mind a bit. She giggled and patted them and hugged and stroked them and rolled with them in the sand and had a swell time. I curled up nearby and watched.

Finally, Faith stood up and announced, "I'm hungry."

"What's the matter?" Bark asked.

"What'd she say?" Woo-Woof asked.

"She wants food," I said.

"Well, you just tell her to follow old Bark!" Bark said and ran off up the beach.

I hadn't yet told him that while I could understand Faith, I couldn't speak to her. But it didn't matter. Faith caught on and raced after him.

"Come on, Eddie!" she called over her shoulder.

I trotted along the beach behind them, feeling a twinge of something. Maybe it was hunger, or dread.

Or jealousy.

16
Om

The electric dogs led us through the jungle, over a small freshwater stream, and up toward the top of a sloping hill, where there was a cave covered by dangling vines. I could see little piles of dirt where they'd buried bones. I smelled markings everywhere.

"This is our den," Bark said proudly.

He disappeared into the cave and reappeared with a portion of a pig carcass. He carried the rotting thing to Faith and presented it to her with a flourish, his tail wagging.

"Yuck!" Faith said, and pinched her nose with her thumb and forefinger.

Bark was crushed.

"What's with her?" Woo-Woof said.

"People are kind of finicky," I explained.

Bark whimpered. He continued to earnestly offer the meat to Faith.

"She doesn't want it," Ro-Ro said to him.

"I'd love a bite, Bark," I said humbly.

"Get your own," he growled.

Faith patted Bark on the head and walked past him into the jungle.

"Let's find some fruit," she said.

We all followed.

The undergrowth was dense and inhabited by many species of butterflies, some as large as the moths back in San Cristóbal de las Casas, which were sometimes as big as bats.

I took this opportunity to speak to Ro-Ro, who seemed friendly and intelligent.

"What do you call this place?" I said.

"Oor-Rr," she said.

"Where are you and your master from?" she asked.

"From Cur-Rr," I said. (Cur-Rr is what electric dogs call Mexico.)

"Where's that?" she asked.

"Across the ocean."

"Oh," she said.

"Have you ever been off Oor-Rr?" I asked.

"No," she said.

I stopped asking questions as a flock of chattering green parrots flew overhead.

"How did you two get here?" Ro-Ro asked.

"In a rocket," I said.

She stopped walking and looked at me.

oor
(Bowwow):
bone

☆

cur
(Bowwow):
electric dog

☆

rr
(Bowwow):
land

"You use a lot of words I don't know," she said.

"It's a thing," I said feebly. "That flies."

"You came from the sky?" she asked.

I nodded.

om
(Bowwow):
light

"Just like Om," she said to herself.

I didn't understand. In Bowwow *om* means "light." We came from the sky like light?

"Bananas!" Faith squealed.

When Ro-Ro and I caught up with her, Faith was shimmying up a banana tree. The other dogs were gathered around the base, talking.

"I think she's terrific," Bark said.

We all looked at him.

"Well she *is*," he said.

"What's with you?" Ro-Ro asked.

"Don't give me that, Ro," Bark said. "I noticed you weren't exactly playing hard to get on the beach. Admit it. There's something about her. Something —"

"Yeah?" Ro-Ro said.

"Something . . . enchanting."

"Oh, brother!" Ro-Ro said.

"Maybe it's her paws," Fruff said.

"Huh?" Ro-Ro said.

"You know. The belly rubs."

"Yeah, yeah," Woo-Woof said, grinning. "The belly rubs."

"It's the thumbs," I said.

"The *what?*" Fruff asked.

"He says they came from the sky," Ro-Ro said to Bark.

"Who says?" Bark asked.

"Grumph," Ro-Ro said. "He says they flew here from across the ocean."

Everyone fell silent.

"Say it again," Bark said.

"In a thing," Ro-Ro said. "A flying thing."

"Like Om!" Fruff said.

Bark wandered away from the group, deep in thought.

"What do you mean?" I asked Fruff. "'Like Om'?"

"Look out below!" Faith hollered from up in the tree. A bunch of bananas thudded on the ground beside us.

"Follow me," Bark said to me. "I'll take you to Om."

So while the others remained with Faith and feasted on bananas and had their bellies rubbed, I followed Bark into the jungle.

"Where you come from, do all the masters fly?" Bark asked as we walked.

I didn't know quite how to answer this. People don't actually fly, as you well know. Flight, for people, requires airplanes or helicopters. Or rocket ships.

"Do all the dogs fly?" he asked before I could think of an answer to his first question.

"No," I said. Of that I was sure.

"Are there birds where you come from?" Bark asked.

"Sure."

We walked in silence awhile.

"You speak Bowwow," I said.

"What's that?"

"Your language," I said. "It's Bowwow. You speak Bowwow."

"I don't get what you mean," Bark said, looking very puzzled.

It was clear that Bark and the other dogs had probably never heard any language besides Bowwow and, I remember thinking, if someone only ever hears one language then it's likely that they assume that their language is the *only* language. To these mutts, the whole notion of language is meaningless. They probably don't even have a word for it, like they didn't for "people" or "rocket ship" or "thumb."

I was about to explain to Bark how there are many languages — both canine and human — when suddenly he stopped.

"This is Om," he said.

We stood before a huge pile of pigs' bones. They had been formed into the shape of a great hound.

"She's our great ancestor," Bark said in a low tone. "The mother of us all. She descended to Oor-Rr from the sky."

"From the sky?" I asked.

Bark didn't answer. He seemed to be meditating.

"How many dogs are there on the island?" I asked.

"What?" he said, emerging from his trance.

"How many dogs are there here, on the island?"

"Not sure," he said.

"But there are others beside you and Ro-Ro and Woo-Woof and Fruff, right?"

"Yeah," Bark said.

"How many more?"

"Don't know."

"Can you speak to them?" I asked.

"Never tried."

"Why not?"

"I just stick to my pack," he said.

"Do they come here to see Om?" I asked.

"Yeah."

"How do you know?"

"Smell."

"Oh," I said. I sat a moment and let all of this sink in.

"Where's your pack?" he asked.

"Back in Cur-Rr," I said. "But we've sort of lost touch since my master came along."

"Don't you have a mate?" Bark asked.

"No," I said. "You?"

"Ro-Ro!" he said, as if he were offended.

"And Woo-Woof and Fruff are —"

"Our puppies," he said.

"I didn't know you were a family," I said.

"A *pack,*" Bark said huffily.

I remembered noticing that when we first encountered the dogs, they didn't engage in the normal circling behavior so common among street dogs. You know, sniffing one another's back ends and growling and all that territorial nonsense. They didn't seem afraid of us, just curious. The knowledge that they were a family cleared up a lot of things for me.

"Are there many dogs where you come from?" Bark asked as we headed back to the others.

"Too many," I replied.

"Do they all have masters?"

"No."

"Well," Bark said wistfully, "yours is wonderful."

17
Message
in a Bottle

When we returned, Woo-Woof and Fruff were sleeping contentedly at Faith's feet. A tall pile of banana peels lay heaped beside them. Faith was playing Fetch with Ro-Ro, and when Bark saw this he quickly joined in on the game.

I pitied them both. I'd been down that road before.

"Edison," Faith said to me. "I've been thinking."

She threw the stick again and Ro-Ro and Bark fell all over each other trying to get it.

"This isn't San Francisco, you know," she said.

Bark returned with the stick and Faith hurled it again.

"I don't know where we are," she said, staring forlornly into space. Then she suddenly brightened. "Why don't we go exploring?"

Ro-Ro and Bark were grappling over the stick. Each

of them held an end of it in their jaws and they were trying to wrestle it away from the other.

"Ready, Eddie?" Faith said, then laughed. "Ready Eddie? Ready Eddie? Eddie, ready?"

I pounced to her feet. I was glad for the attention.

Ro-Ro and Bark dropped the stick and rushed to us when they saw we were leaving.

"Woo-Woof! Fruff!" Bark barked.

The two puppies awoke and scampered after us.

"Let's follow the beach," Faith said, "so we don't get lost."

The low winter sun shone brightly. The sky was cloudless and the sea was brilliant blue. Sometimes fear and confusion can blunt your perceptions. You become so driven to make sense of things, to identify the dangers lurking around the next corner, that you neglect to see the wonders all around you. As we walked, I realized I'd never set foot on a beach, not before yesterday. I liked the sensation of my paws sinking deep into the warm sand. I enjoyed playing with the waves, chasing them out, being chased back in.

From the beach, the sea looked as if it went on forever. It stretched out as far as you could see and then appeared to evaporate into the sky.

I wondered how many water dishes it would fill.

I was thirsty!

I dove into the surf and swallowed a snoutful of water, and immediately wished I hadn't. Live and learn.

I could see that Faith was enjoying herself and I imagined I knew why. Everything I knew about oceans and beaches and such I'd learned from her stories about San Francisco, California. No, we were not in San Francisco. But I guess a beach is a beach is a beach.

We walked along the beach, around the bone's extremities to its long shaft.

(Perhaps I should explain, dear reader, since you may not be an expert on bones as I am. A bone is comprised of three basic parts — the long, narrow shaft and the two bumpy extremities on either end. Since Oor-Rr was bone-shaped, I took to referring to its different areas as the extremities and the shaft.)

Halfway down the shaft, with the far extremities well within sight, Faith stopped and said, "I need to rest."

And so we all lay down on the beach in a close bunch and soaked up the sun and listened to the surf. I was gradually being seduced by the island, by its open spaces and its streetlessness. It was heavenly just lying there, without a care or worry in the world. I even forgot my hunger and thirst. Soon we had all drifted off to sleep.

When I awoke, the sun was just setting over the extremities that we'd left behind. I decided then to name them the Western Extremities.

I awoke first. Ro-Ro and Bark were snugly curled into Faith's armpits, their heads resting on her chest.

Woo-Woof and Fruff were nuzzled in at her shoulders. I'd slept between her feet, not wishing to engage in this most-prized-pooch contest. It was beneath me. After all, I was Faith's true pet, her first and foremost electric dog.

Or so I kept telling myself.

The tide had reached us and it wasn't long before it had awakened Faith. She sat up, stretched, and yawned. This roused the hounds.

"Almost nightfall," Ro-Ro said, yawning, her long tongue curling like a tail.

"Better be heading back," Bark said.

"What's that?" Faith said, pointing out to sea.

We all turned and looked. A bright blue glass bottle was washing up on the beach. The old retrieval instinct in me, and the new ones in Ro-Ro and Bark, sent the three of us scrambling into the waves. I, the more experienced retriever, emerged victorious and carried the bottle back to my master. I did not do so without strutting.

The bottle was square and plugged with a cork.

"Do you suppose . . . ?" Faith said.

She popped the cork and peeked in.

"Eddie!" she said. "There's a note!"

She shook the bottle, and fished in first with her fingers and then with a stick, until finally she extracted a rolled-up scrap of paper.

She hurriedly unrolled it and read it aloud:

*To Whom It May Concern, though by now I
am almost certain that no one is concerned.*

*I am stuck on an island. I have been here
a very long time. When I arrived here I was
young. Now I am old. I am very lonely. The
island is in the Pacific Ocean, though I can't
say exactly where. I can only say that it is
shaped like a bone.*

Please rescue me, if you're not too busy.

Sincerely,
Beverly Sinclair Glum

"What is it?" Bark asked. "What's she saying?"

"It's a note," I said. I didn't expect them to understand, but I was too deep in thought to explain.

Faith fiddled her lower lip and thought and
thought and thought. I caught on before she did, and
waited for her to catch up.

"She must have written the note," she said, "put it
in the bottle, and then thrown it into the sea. The tide
must've carried it back in."

She scratched her head and rubbed her chin. She
began to smile. She was getting it.

"Eddie," she said. "Beverly's *here*!"

I agreed completely. The likelihood of another
bone-shaped island in the vicinity seemed remote at
best.

I also noted, by the by, that the note was written in

English. I'm not sure the significance of that fact struck Faith. Like Bark, and most creatures, Faith only notices language when it's different from her own.

"What's going on?" Bark demanded.

I explained to him what was happening and was unsurprised to learn that the dogs didn't know that people had a system by which they could represent their language on paper. Writing and reading were completely new concepts to them, and it was not easy getting them to understand. Still, it was quite reasonable that it was difficult for them. Until the day before, they had not even known there were such things as people.

"We must find Beverly!" Faith proclaimed.

"You're saying that there might be another creature like your master on the island?" Ro-Ro asked me.

"Yes," I said.

"Where?" Bark asked.

"Oh, Bark!" Ro-Ro said. "How would he know?"

"I don't know," I said.

"Let's go look down there," Faith said, pointing toward the Eastern Extremities.

"Does she see it?" Bark asked. He sounded a bit afraid.

"Does she see what?" I asked.

"The other master," he said.

"No," I said. "She said that maybe the one who wrote the note lives down there, that's all."

"It's possible," Ro-Ro said. "We never go there."

"That's because I've heard the cries of wolves coming from there before," Bark said. "It could be dangerous."

I whined.

"It's okay, boy," Faith said. "Don't be afraid."

She crouched down and gave me a hug. Then she stood and said, *"¡Vámonos!"*

¡Vámonos!
(Spanish):
Let's go!

18
Pork

Within the hour, the sun had set and darkness had swept the island. With no man-made lights of any kind — no streetlights, or headlights, or house lights — night on the island was pitch-black, with the exception of the twinkling stars and the moon. That night the moon was shaped like fangs.

"I guess we'd better stop and sleep," Faith said. "It's too dark to see anything."

She sat down on the sand. The five of us surrounded her.

"I'm hungry," she said.

I hadn't eaten all day.

"And tired," she continued. "And cold."

"What does she want?" Bark asked.

"Food," I told him. "And sleep, and warmth."

Bark rose to his feet, licked Faith's face, and said, "Keep her warm. I'll go find food."

"But what about the w-wolves?" Woo-Woof asked.

"Don't worry about me, son," Bark said, stiffening his spine. "I'll be right back with supper."

"I'll go with you," someone said.

Do you know who it was, dear reader, who so bravely offered to go with Bark into the dark jungle? Can you guess? It was I, Edison the electric dog.

Hunger makes one do strange things.

What by day had been a vibrant and beautiful place became sinister under cover of night. Suddenly everything in the jungle seemed alive, and hungry. The cool night air was roaring with the sounds of pestilent insects, venomous reptiles, and carnivorous wild animals.

"Has it occurred to you," Bark said, "that this other master might be Om's master?"

"Om had a master?" I asked.

"I don't know," he said. "I sort of remember being told that she did, but I wouldn't have known what a master was then, so I didn't give it much thought."

"How long ago was it that Om descended from the sky?" I asked.

"You mean, how many days?"

"Well, yes, I suppose," I said. I guess I couldn't really expect him to have a concept of years.

"Shoot, I don't know," he said. "A lot!"

I heard a rustle in the brush to my right.

"Sssshh!" Bark said.

I shushed.

We stood still. I didn't breathe.

"Okay," Bark said finally. "Come on."

"Was it wolves?" I asked timidly. I'd had no experience with wolves before, you see, dear reader, so I was relying on Bark's nose to smell them out.

"Maybe," he said.

I followed closely behind him. *Very* closely.

"So your master can't understand you when you talk?" he asked.

"No, she can't."

"But you can understand her?"

"Uh-huh."

"But she doesn't know you can understand her?"

"That's right."

"No?" he asked.

"No," I said, irritated. "She doesn't know I understand her."

"Do all the dogs where you come from understand people?"

"Not all of them," I said. "People don't all speak the same language."

"Do all the people understand each other?"

"No," I said. I understood and appreciated his natural curiosity. After all, this language stuff was new to him. Still, I was busy listening for wolves and starving to death, and his persistent yammering was really beginning to bug me.

"Do all the dogs understand each other?" he asked.

I shook my head.

"But you understand me, right?" he said.

I stopped walking.

"Yes, Bark," I said testily. "I understand you. Isn't that obvious?"

"Huh? Oh. Yeah," he said. "I guess it is."

"Isn't that a banana tree?" I asked, pointing.

"No, it isn't," he said. "So let me get this straight. Not all dogs speak the same language, right?"

"Right."

"But you and I speak the same language, right?"

"Obviously."

"Well, don't you think that's kind of strange?" he said. "I mean, what are the chances?"

"I admit," I said, "that I thought it was odd when —"

"Sssshh!" Bark interrupted.

I shut my yap and froze.

"Wolves?" I whispered.

"Sssshh!" Bark said again.

His ears perked up and pivoted.

"What's her name?" he whispered.

"Who?" I whispered back, perplexed.

"Your master," he said.

"What about the wolves?" I asked.

"Must have imagined it," he said, walking again. "What's her name?"

I closed my eyes and took a breath. My heart was fluttering. My throat was parched. My stomach was growling. I was not happy.

"Are you sure there's nothing out there?" I asked.

"Almost," he said. "Come on."

"Well?" he asked after we'd walked a bit. "What's her name?"

"I can't say it in Bowwow," I said. "It's a people name, a people sound. She doesn't have a Bowwow name."

Bark thought for a second.

"I know," he said. "Let's call her *Bock Ru-Fuff*!"

I snickered and then he chuckled, and suddenly we were both laughing our heads off.

"Sssshh!" Bark said suddenly, and put his paw over my snout.

I was petrified. Perhaps we were being stalked, I thought. I tried to speak.

"Sssshh!" Bark repeated.

He took his paw away and got down into an attack position. His fur stood on end. His fangs gleamed.

"Pig," he whispered.

I smelled it then.

"Do they have horns?" I whispered.

"Sssshh!"

"Well *you* talked," I said.

bock
(Bowwow):
parrot
☆
ru
(Bowwow):
without
☆
fuff
(Bowwow):
feathers

"SSSSHH!" he hissed.

"Okay, okay," I whispered.

What happened next happened so fast that I could not possibly describe it as quickly as it occurred. Fortunately for you, dear reader, I am relating this story after the fact, so I can slow it down for you.

I heard a rustle of leaves to my left, and when I glanced over, a small, black pig rushed out of the brush behind Bark, in front of me. It darted across my path and careened into the brush to my right. Before Bark could even spin around to see what it was, another pig burst out of the brush, crossed before me, and disappeared, just as the previous one had done.

"What was that?" Bark asked.

Before I could answer, yet another one shot between us and was gone.

"Come on!" Bark yelped. He plunged headlong into the brush after the third little pig.

I stood dazed for a second, then joined in on the chase.

As we were racing after the pigs, I began to long for those dry, tasteless kibbles that Milagros poured into my dog dish each day. At least with kibbles I needn't chase my dinner through a creepy, wolf-infested jungle in the middle of the night. Kibbles just sit and wait for you. They're meek and lifeless and they don't have horns. There is a world of difference between kibbles and wild pigs, I can tell you.

We'd plowed through the dense underbrush in pursuit of these pigs for quite some time when I began to question whether or not Bark was still onto their scent.

"Bark!" I said.

"Yeah?" he said, panting.

"You still smell them?"

"Just keep up!"

"I can't," I said. "I've got to rest."

"No!" he said. "We're gaining on 'em."

Just then a pig shot across our path in front of me, behind Bark.

"Bark!" I yelled.

Another pig crossed the path, this time behind me.

"Bark!" I yelled again.

"Shut up and come on!" he snapped.

He hadn't seen them.

"But Bark —"

A third pig burst out of the brush. This one clipped Bark's backside and sent him spinning off the path onto his face.

He jumped to his feet, snarling, and shoved his snout close into mine.

"What's with you?" he growled.

"What?" I said, recoiling.

"Watch where you're going!"

"It wasn't me. It was —"

Thankfully, a fourth pig darted between us just then, right under Bark's chin.

Bark clearly had a notion to pounce into the brush after it, but he held up.

"Forget it," he said.

We both collapsed on the ground.

"Where are we?" I asked.

"Not sure," he said.

"Not sure?"

"Yeah. Not sure. What of it? I'll get us back to the beach."

"What about food?"

"Does Bock Ru-Fuff like papaya?" Bark asked.

"Yeah, I think so."

"Well, we passed some a while back," he said. "We can probably scrounge up some bones for us dogs."

"Hey!" I said.

"What?"

"Smell *that,*" I said, rising to my feet.

Bark sniffed.

"Yeah, yeah," he said. "I smell it. Smells good. What is it?"

You'd never guess what it was, dear reader. It was *carnitas! ¡Qué milagro!* Like a dream come true! I had not been starving in vain!

"It's pork," I said. "Roast pork glazed with fat." I licked my chops.

¡Qué milagro!
(Spanish):
*What a
miracle!*

Bark looked puzzled.

Remember, dear reader, for your benefit I'm telling this story in English. I'm assuming that you can read English, otherwise you wouldn't have gotten this far. Also, remember that the electric dogs on Oor-Rr could not understand English. All of our conversations were in Bowwow, but, for your sake, I have translated them into English. Lastly, remember that these dogs lived far away from what people call civilization and that many concepts that we understand very well (like automobiles or ice cream) were totally unknown to them.

As always, I'd spoken to Bark in Bowwow. I'd said *carnitas* in Bowwow: *grouk rork.*

grouk
(Bowwow):
roasted

☆

rork
(Bowwow):
pork

I learned that Bark understood "pork" only too well. It was the core of his diet. It was the "roast" part that had thrown him, and I soon figured out why.

Dogs don't cook.

People do.

"Bark!" I said, with a jump.

"What?! What?!" he said. The poor beast was terribly confused.

"Cooking!" I said. "I smell cooking!"

"What are you babbling about?" he said.

"Don't you get it?" I said. "Of course you don't. It doesn't matter. I'll explain later."

"No!" he barked. "Now!"

"PEOPLE!" I hollered. "HERE!"

19
Beverly Sinclair Glum

I n all honesty, I'm not sure whether it was curiosity
or *carnitas* that so strongly drew me to Beverly Sinclair Glum. Let's call it a tie.

We followed the scent through the jungle to a
clearing. In the center of the clearing was an open
fire. Over the fire, skewered and suspended, was a
sumptuous, sizzling slab of pork.

An old man emerged from a small cave beyond the
fire. He had long white hair that reached down his
back to his bottom, and, in front, a beard that reached
nearly as low. Squeezed between these two great
masses of dingy, wiry hair blinked two red eyes, blue
in the center. His clothes were made primarily of
leaves and grasses sewn together by braids of stems
and vines. His torso was scrawny and his skin, leath-
ery. His ribs stuck out, not unlike, I thought, most
electric dogs I knew.

He sat on a rock by the fire and gave the pork a half turn.

We'd perched on a ridge just above the camp. Bark hunkered down on the ground.

"Is that a people?" he whispered.

"Yes."

"But it has so much fur."

"Some have more than others," I said.

"What's that?" Bark asked.

"What?"

"That sound?"

It was the old man. His lips were puckered and a wheezy sound was passing through them. I could make out a lilting little tune. It was quite charming, actually. Then, in a weak, raspy voice he recited a nursery rhyme:

> "Bow wow wow
>   Whose dog art thou?
>   'Little Tommy Tinker's dog,
>   Bow wow wow.'
>   Tell tale, tit!
>   Your tongue shall be slit,
>   And all the dogs in our town
>   Shall have a little bit."

Then he chortled and coughed and turned the pork again.

"Do you think this is the one who threw the bottle into the sea?" Bark whispered.

Before I could answer, the old man suddenly rose to his feet, turned, and walked to his cave.

"Did he hear us?" Bark whispered.

I shrugged. (Yes, we shrug. Dogs shrug.)

When he emerged again he had something in his hand, a small wooden object that looked familiar to me. There was a long, dangling piece of string attached to it. He bent over forward, very slowly, and picked up a small stone.

And then I knew exactly what he had, dear reader. It was a *tirador*!

"Run!" I yelled.

"Beat it, you mangy curs!" the old man croaked, and fired in our direction.

The pebble came sailing in at us just over our heads. We hightailed it until we were at what we considered a safe distance away, then lay panting.

"What was that?" Bark asked.

I explained to him all about *tiradores* (we call them *pip-pips* in Bowwow) and how they were commonly used in Mexico, especially by young boys upon poor, hapless girls and electric dogs.

"Cur-Rr sounds like a dangerous place," Bark said.

"It is," I said. "But it's home."

tiradores
(Spanish):
slingshots

☆

pip-pips
(Bowwow):
slingshots

I suggested that we go back and get the others, and Bark agreed.

"But first," I said — and I still can't believe I really said this — "let's get the *grouk rork*."

I could, of course, pretend that swiping the *carnitas* was a very daring thing to do, but it was actually quite simple. One of us — in this case, Bark (it was my plan) — went around behind the old man's camp and began yowling. This attracted the old guy — and his *tirador* — from his dinner long enough for the other — in this case, me — to steal in, grab the grub, and flee. Like I said, simple.

But to hear Bark tell it . . .

"And then," Bark said to his family when we returned, "he raised his *pip-pip* and fired — *ZZZING!* The stone came a hair's breadth from cracking my skull!"

"Ooooh!" Woo-Woof said, impressed.

Of course, Faith couldn't understand any of Bark's tall tale. She just ate her supper.

After we'd all eaten, we cuddled up together and slept. Perhaps we should have headed out right then to the camp, but, frankly, I was bushed, and the way I had it figured, the old man would probably still be there come morning.

In the morning, Bark and I were able to pick up our trail from the night before and lead the group quickly to the camp. We had a bit of trouble conveying to Faith the urgency of heading into the jungle, as opposed to continuing along the beach, but after some tugging and whining, she saw things our way.

"Now stay quiet," Bark said to his kin as we neared the camp. "Remember the *pip-pip*."

Faith must have recognized the camp for what it was right off, even without the presence of the old man.

"Good boy, Eddie!" she said loudly.

Bark glowered at her. Woo-Woof and Fruff dove into the underbrush and covered their eyes with their paws.

But I didn't. Somehow I felt safer with Faith there and I guess Ro-Ro did, too, for she remained standing beside me.

"This must be Beverly's house," Faith said. "I wonder if she's home."

She? I remember thinking.

Faith stepped through the brush into the clearing. I felt more secure with her around, as I said, but not so secure as to actually wander into camp with her. After all, the man had fired a dangerous weapon at me. No, Ro-Ro and I stayed with the others at the clearing's edge.

"Hello?" Faith called. "Anybody home?"

No answer.

"Hello-oh," she called again.

Nothing.

She poked around the camp, noticing the metal pots and utensils, the bamboo lean-to, and the *tirador,* which the old man had left on a rock. She picked it up.

"She's got the *pip-pip!*" Bark whispered.

Now that my master was armed, I decided to join her in the fray. The others followed.

"It looks just like the ones they sell in the *mercado,*" Faith said to me.

She was right. *Indígenas* commonly carved the handles of their *tiradores* into the shapes of animals — birds, jaguars, people. The handle of the old man's *tirador* was jaguar-shaped.

Electric dogs. Bowwow. Descents from the sky. Notes in English. A *tirador* in the shape of a jaguar. It was all a little too coincidental, I thought. Spooky, even.

Faith moved over to the cave entrance.

"Hello-oh!" she called in. Her voice echoed. "Anybody home?"

She poked her head inside.

"Oh!" she said with a start.

She backed away from the entrance. From the shadows of the cave, the old man appeared.

20
Luz

His eyes were glossy and his lower lip, which was dried and flaky, trembled as if he were too scared to speak but nevertheless wished to. He braced himself against the cave entrance with his hand. His knees wobbled and knocked together. What skinny legs he had!

"Hi," Faith said.

The old guy shrank away a little. He opened his mouth, but nothing came out. With effort he was able to produce a low, croaky sound.

"I'm Faith and this is my dog, Edison," Faith said.

I gave him a nod.

The old man didn't look at me, so intent was he on Faith. He looked as if he was seeing a dream made flesh. Or a ghost.

Faith pulled the blue bottle out of her pocket and,

upon sight of it, the old man reached out his hand and let out a long moan.

"I found this on the beach," Faith said. "It was written by an old woman named Beverly who's stranded on a bone-shaped island and —"

"N-n-no," the old man said. He closed his eyes and shook his head.

Faith squinted at him, and, unconsciously, began shaking her head slightly, too.

"No?" she asked.

The old man continued to shake his head. He withdrew his outstretched hand back toward his body and, with a quivering, crooked forefinger, pointed to his own chest.

"You?" Faith said.

He nodded.

"I am . . ." he said hoarsely, then coughed, took a breath, and began again. "I am . . . Beverly . . ."

"You?" Faith said again.

". . . Sinclair . . ." he continued.

"Glum!" Faith finished, pop-eyed.

"Indeed," Beverly Sinclair Glum said with a nod.

Faith and I each took a deep breath and then sighed.

"But," Faith said, with her hands on her hips, "isn't Beverly a girl's name?"

Mr. Glum opened his mouth to speak but once again nothing came out. His brow furrowed (again, he reminded me of an electric dog), and he stepped toward us, out of the cave, into the sunlight. A shadow of a smile flashed on his face.

"Sometimes," he said.

"I don't mean to be rude," Faith said quickly. "I've just never heard of a boy named Beverly before."

"Sit," Beverly said.

"It's a perfectly *fine* name," Faith went on, then asked, "What?"

"Have a seat," Beverly said.

"Oh. Thank you," Faith said and sat down on a rock. We dogs scurried around behind her.

Beverly sat down on another one, facing Faith.

"I'm from San Francisco," Faith said.

"Never been there," Beverly said.

I could tell from his accent that he was British, like the woman who had helped Faith that day in the *mercado*. He said "been" like "bean."

"How old are you?" Faith asked.

"Not quite sure," Beverly said. He scratched his head.

"When were you born?"

"In December. December the seventeenth, I believe."

"No, no. What *year* were you born?"

He closed his eyes and then closed his bony fingers over them.

"1942, I believe," he said, lowering his hands. "No, it was 1924. Yes, that's it. 1924. I'm sure of it."

"You know what?" Faith said, and then stopped to count on her fingers. "Yes. *Today* is December seventeenth!"

Beverly looked unfazed. He shrugged a little.

"Don't you get it, Bev?" Faith said. "It's your birthday. Today's your birthday!"

Beverly's eyes widened a bit. His mouth fell open.

"In fact!" Faith said excitedly. "It's your *seventieth* birthday today!"

"My birthday?" he said. His voice was colored with many emotions. I detected disbelief, confusion, regret, surprise, sadness. He sat quietly, staring off, and Faith, as if she knew that he needed the time, let him be.

"I'm sev —" he said finally, then swallowed hard. Tears came to his eyes. "I'm seventy."

"Yes!" Faith said, jumping to her feet. She slapped him on the shoulder. "Seventy today!"

"Seventy," Beverly muttered.

"Happy birthday, Bev," Faith said, beaming.

"Thank you, Faith," Beverly said. "I haven't had a birthday in, oh, quite some time."

"Naw, Bev, you had one every year. You just didn't know it."

"I guess you're right," he said.

"How old were you when you came here?" Faith asked.

"Ten," Beverly answered immediately.

I remember wondering if he'd fancied himself to be ten ever since.

"Then you've been here sixty years," Faith said and shook her head. "Wow."

"Wow," Beverly repeated somberly.

"And there's never been another person on this island before?" Faith asked.

"Not that I've ever been aware of," Beverly said.

"You've spent almost your whole life here, then," Faith said.

"Yes," Beverly said. "I have."

Despite how old it was, and how much hair covered it, his face looked like that of a little boy. I imagined that Faith was thinking the same thing as she gazed at him, especially when she crouched before him on the ground and put her arms across his lap and looked up into his eyes. He began to weep.

"You must have been pretty lonely," Faith said.

Bev sniffed hard and wiped his nose with his beard.

"Yes," he said. "I suppose I must have been."

"Poor baby," Faith said and patted him on the shoulder. "Well, you won't be lonely anymore. Either we'll find a way off this island, or we'll both stay here stranded. Either way you won't be alone anymore."

She looked over at me.

"Me and Eddie will keep you company," she said.

"He came with you?" Beverly said through his sobs.

"Uh-huh," Faith said.

Beverly grew strangely preoccupied. He stared at a point off to my left. I turned to see what it was he was looking at. It was Ro-Ro. He looked at her as if he hadn't noticed her before.

"Why is he staring at me?" Ro-Ro asked.

"I don't know," I said.

"What's wrong, Beverly?" Faith asked. "What is it?"

She turned and looked at Ro-Ro, too.

"All right," Ro-Ro said. "What's going on? Somebody better tell me why everyone's gawking at me, or I'm gonna bite someone."

"I came here with a dog, too," Beverly said.

"You did?" Faith said.

"Yes," he said. "A black dog."

I quickly filled Ro-Ro and the others in on what had been said.

(And maybe I should remind you, dear reader, that Ro-Ro has a coat the color of charcoal.)

"He must be dead by now," Faith said.

"Yes," Beverly said, then shook his head and said, "No."

"No?" Faith asked. "He's alive?"

"No, I'm sure she's quite dead," Beverly said. "But

it was a she. My dog was a she. Not a he. She was a she. A girl dog. Luz. Her name was Luz."

"Loose?" Faith asked. "Like, 'my tooth is loose'?"

"No, no," Beverly said. "Luz. L-U-Z. It's a Spanish name. It means 'light.' I got her in Mexico. In Palenque. She was just a puppy when I got her. You can imagine my surprise when, after a few weeks here, she had puppies of her own."

"Your puppy had puppies?" Faith asked.

"I guess she was older than I thought," Beverly said.

"I'm very sorry she's dead," Faith said.

Beverly wasn't listening. He was staring at Ro-Ro again.

"Well?" Ro-Ro said.

"His dog had puppies," I said quickly, so as not to miss any of the people's conversation. "I think maybe he thinks you're one of the puppies, but he's too old and you're too young for that to be true."

"What was his dog's name?" Bark asked.

I couldn't say Luz in Bowwow — it's a people word — so I translated its meaning ("light") to Bowwow, and couldn't believe my ears.

"Om," I said. "His dog's name was Om!"

luz
(Spanish):
light

21
Bev's Tale

All of the coincidences were now explained. Everything had fallen into place.

Beverly and Luz had come to the island together. Beverly had gotten Luz in Mexico. Obviously, she was an electric dog and spoke Bowwow. She'd had puppies on the island and taught them to speak Bowwow, too. Her puppies must have had puppies and they in turn must have had puppies and they in turn must have had puppies and grand-puppies. She, as Bark had said, was the great ancestor, the mother of them all. It seemed to me completely likely, maybe even certain, that Bark and Ro-Ro were great-great-great-grandpuppies of Luz (or Om, as they call her) and that Fruff and Woo-Woof were her great-great-great-(great?)-grandpuppies. In any case, they were all related, all family.

Now, dear reader, let me assure you that this tale, as

tall as it may seem, is absolutely true. I admit, to suggest that not only did two English-speaking children both end up marooned on the same remote, deserted island, but that they had also both brought with them electric dogs does sound rather hard to believe. But it's true. If it's not, may I never again savor another morsel of *carnitas*.

I explained to Ro-Ro how Beverly had brought Luz (Om) to the island (Oor-Rr) from Mexico (Cur-Rr) — (oh dear, this *is* confusing!) — and how Luz had had puppies there.

"What happened to them?" Ro-Ro asked me.

"What happened to the puppies?" Faith asked Beverly.

"Wait a sec," I told Ro-Ro. "He's about to explain."

Beverly looked away from Ro-Ro and looked into Faith's eyes, then stared down at the ground. He did this for a long time, until I thought he'd fallen asleep.

"Bev?" Faith said, touching his knee.

Beverly lifted his head. Tears streaked down his cheeks.

"I chased them away," he said.

"Why?" Faith said with a gasp.

Beverly looked over at Ro-Ro again. I explained to her what he'd just said.

"Oh! The brute!" she said, and snarled.

"It's all right, Bev," Faith said, patting Ro-Ro. "She's a friend of Eddie's and mine. She won't hurt you."

"I need to go in now," Beverly said, and stood.

"Wait, Bev," Faith said. "Don't go yet."

"No, I must," he said. He walked over to the cave and went in.

Faith followed but stayed just outside the entrance.

"Beverly?" she called softly. "Beverly?"

"Go away!" Beverly called from inside. "Leave me alone!"

"Oh, Beverly," Faith said. "Don't be like that. I'm your friend. Don't be afraid."

"I'm not afraid."

"No, no, of course you're not. Let me come in, Bev. I just want to talk. I'll leave the dogs out here."

There was no answer.

"Bev, it's your birthday. You don't want to be alone on your birthday, do you?"

Silence.

"Bev?"

"All right," he said at last. "But leave the dogs outside."

She turned to us and said in a stern voice, "Now you dogs *stay*!" and then winked.

After she went in, I curled up by the cave door and listened.

"I was scared," Beverly said from inside.

"Scared?" Faith asked.

"I was all alone here, just me and Luz. I'd never been all alone before."

"I understand," Faith said.

"I didn't even know Luz was expecting puppies. Suddenly I had five dogs instead of one. I didn't know how to feed them, to take care of them. I was frightened. So one day . . ."

His voice trailed off.

"It's okay," Faith said.

"So one day," he continued, "I walked them to the other side of the island, and I . . . I . . ."

"You ditched them?"

"Yeah."

"Luz, too?"

"I hadn't intended to, but she went with them," Beverly said. "She went with her pups."

"And you never saw them again?"

"No, never. I see dogs around now sometimes. I feel so bad. I chase them off."

As Beverly and Faith talked, I translated for the others.

"The creep," Bark said. "I ought to chew his leg to ribbons."

"Oh, give him a break, will you, Bark?" Ro-Ro said.

"He sounds sweet," Woo-Woof said.

"Sweet?" Bark said. "Maybe you'd feel differently if he'd shot stones at *your* thick skull!"

"I'm not thick," Woo-Woof said.

"That's right," Ro-Ro said to Bark. "He's not."

"Quiet!" I said. "I can't hear."

"How'd you get here?" Faith asked Beverly.

"Balloon," he said.

"Balloon?"

"Yes. You see, my father, Shirley Glum —"

"Your father's name is Shirley?" Faith interrupted, giggling.

"Y-yes. Why? Is that funny?"

"Never mind," Faith said, and suppressed her laughter.

"Anyway, as I was saying, my daddy was very rich, you see. He was an achaelogicist . . . an arcolegiast . . ."

"An archaeologist?" Faith asked.

"Why, yes. Have you heard of him?"

"No," Faith said.

"Well, he dug for bones and pots and things, you know. That was his job. So one day he comes home from work and says to my mother, 'Darling, we're off to Mexico,' and she says, 'Really? How nice.'

"So we moved to Palenque — do you know where that is? Well, no matter. It's a dreadfully dull place. Hot as blazes. My father was excavating old pyramids and temples, I think. The Mayans. I was terribly bored, mostly. He knew it. He used to buy me things to keep me pacified. Anything I asked for, he'd get. He ordered stuff from London and had it shipped. Archery sets, BB guns, slingshots. Whatever I wanted.

"He knew that I hated living in Mexico. Horrid place. Ever been? Ghastly. I don't know if you know this but they barely speak English there at all. Truly. Just Spanish and some stupid Indian languages. Terrible! And nothing to do all day long. No rugby or cricket or circuses. I wanted to go home. Back to England."

Faith had fallen strangely silent.

"So one day I asked my father for a miniature hot-air balloon. It was pretty difficult to get, and very expensive, too, but he managed it. He ordered it from the States, I think. Took over a month to get it. I told him it was just for fun. A hobby. He did anything for me, my old man. Anything. He was a good egg."

A funny tone entered Beverly's voice as he said that last sentence.

"I imagine he's dead now," he said.

"Yeah," Faith said.

"My mother, too, I expect."

"My father's dead," Faith said.

"He is?"

"Uh-huh. He got real sick and died."

"Sorry."

"Thanks," Faith said.

They both sat quietly awhile, then Faith spoke.

"My mother married another man," she said. "Hector. A Mexican."

"Ew! A Mexican?" Beverly said. "Too bad!"

"He is not 'too bad,'" Faith said angrily. "He's terrific. He's nice and sweet and lovable. And nice."

"Sorry. I only thought —"

"Well, just watch it," Faith said. "I have lots of friends who are Mexicans."

"You do?"

"Yes, I do," she said. "Like Coco, and Señor Latas and Milagros, and Edison."

Yeah!

"I'm really terribly sorry, Faith," Beverly said. "Please forgive me."

They got quiet again and I took the opportunity to fill the dogs in on what had been said.

"So you and Luz flew here in your hot-air balloon?" Faith asked finally.

"Yes. Not intentionally, of course. I meant to end up in London."

"What happened?"

"You just can't trust balloons. They seem to go wherever they like and then take their dear sweet time getting there."

"So you sailed west instead of east?"

"Yes, I suppose so. Then we got caught in a storm and, if you can believe it, a seagull flew right into the balloon and punctured it!"

"Really?"

"Really. We dropped into the sea and swam here to

the island," Beverly said. "And I've been here ever since."

He took a deep breath and then asked, "And, pray tell, how did you end up here?"

Faith answered but, well, I missed it. I must have dozed off.

I knew the story anyway.

22
The *Peahen* Again

"**W**ake up, Grumph! Wake up!"

It was Fruff.

"Look!"

Faith and Beverly had left the cave and were leaving the camp. I hurried after them.

"Hey, buddy," Faith said to me as I caught up. "Wanna go for a walk with us?"

Yes, I did, as did the others.

As we walked, Beverly described all that we saw. He did so with great pride despite the fact that the names he used for many of the fruit and flowers were clearly incorrect. He called a fuchsia a "firebell" and a guava a "finkleberry."

"I didn't know the real names so I just made them up," he explained coyly.

We followed the beach around the first hump of

the Eastern Extremities. The coast became rockier and rose up into high cliffs.

"So you've never seen TV?" Faith asked.

"Not even sure I understand what it is," Beverly answered.

"Do you know there have been people on the moon?" Faith asked.

"You don't say," Beverly said. "Well, what do you know about that. How'd they do that then?"

"Rockets."

"Oh. Like yours?"

"Yeah," Faith said proudly. "Like mine."

"Do people still drive automobiles?" Beverly asked.

"Sure," Faith said.

"I never drove one," Beverly said sadly.

"Me, either," Faith said.

Beverly smiled.

"What are they talking about?" Bark asked.

I did not wish to stop and explain all about television and automobiles and trips to the moon, so I just said, "The weather."

"Was Luz an electric dog?" Faith asked.

Beverly chuckled.

"Yes, yes, she was," he said. *"Una perra eléctrica.* I'd forgotten. And Edison? He's electric, yes?"

Faith smiled and nodded.

"These dogs are electric, too," Beverly said.

"I think they like you," Faith said.

Beverly bent slightly at the knees and patted Woo-Woof, who had been walking closely behind him.

"Good girl," he said.

"It's a boy," Faith said.

"Really?" Beverly said. "What's his name?"

"Doesn't have one."

"Let's call him Shirley," Beverly said, and grinned.

"I said it's a *boy,* Bev," Faith said, laughing. "You still want to go home, don't you? Back to England?" Faith asked.

"I don't really know," Beverly said dreamily.

"What about the bottle? The note?"

"Oh, that," he said. "Occasionally a bottle washes up on shore. I still have bits of paper lying about. So I scribble a note and toss it out to sea. When I was younger I used to imagine that someone might find one of them and come and rescue me. But not anymore. Now I do it out of habit. It's something to do. A game I play with myself. I'm so old now. There's no one to go back to. This is my home."

He gazed out over the ocean, his long hair and beard blowing in the breeze.

"I don't know, Faith," he said. "I just don't think I'd fit in back there now."

Faith hooked his arm in hers and drew him close.

"Sad face," she said, and frowned, then sang:

"Uh rum sum sum

Uh rum sum sum

Gooey gooey gooey gooey rum sum sum

Uh ramby

Uh ramby

Gooey gooey gooey gooey rum sum sum!"

Beverly clapped. "Bravo! Bravo!"

Faith bowed.

"Thank you, thank you," she said. "You're too kind."

"I don't understand it, though," Beverly said.

"Me, either," Faith said. "But I like it."

It was at that exact moment that I saw her.

I looked up, and there she was.

I recognized her immediately, of course.

I barked an alarm and tore off down the beach toward her. She was wedged into some rocks.

"Eddie!" Faith yelled, running after me. "What is it?"

The electric dogs were right at my heels. Beverly went as fast as he could, which wasn't fast, but which wasn't as slow as you'd think.

"Eddie!" Faith yelled. "Eddie!"

I couldn't believe my eyes, but there she was — banged up and broken down but still in one piece.

"The *Peahen*!" Faith screamed when she'd spotted her.

Yes, the *Peahen* had landed.

☆　　☆　　☆

Faith and Beverly dragged her up onto the beach and set her upright. This was not easy and left poor Beverly huffing and puffing and moaning, flat on his back on the sand. Faith went in to check the damage. She groaned a lot. Then she came out holding a soggy *Higglety Pigglety Pop!* and a plastic bag filled with jalapeños.

"It's a physical impossibility," she said.

"Are you sure?" Beverly said, sitting up.

Faith didn't answer. She sank down into the sand, buried her face in her hands, and cried.

"There, there now," Beverly said, moving over beside her. "Don't do that. Please. It's not as bad as all that. Surely. We'll get her all fixed up, good as new. You'll see."

"No!" Faith yelled into her hands. "It's hopeless! Hopeless, hopeless, hopeless, hopeless!"

Beverly seemed unsure of what to do. He patted her back, but then stopped and brought his hand to his mouth, and then started patting her head. He looked around as if he were looking for someone to help him.

"What's the matter with her?" asked Ro-Ro. "What's she doing?"

"She's crying," I said. "She says the rocket won't work, that we can't use it to get off the island."

"Is it true?" Bark asked.

"I don't know," I said. "I don't know how it works."

"Is this what you came down from the sky in?" Fruff asked.

I was beginning to grow impatient with their questions. I was watching Faith, and thinking.

"Are you —" Bark began to ask.

"Leave me alone!" I barked and walked away.

"Well," Bark said behind me, "what's with him?"

I climbed up on a rock and looked far off into the distance. Chiapas, my home, lay beyond my vision, and I could see farther than I'd ever seen before. California, I imagined, was just as far in another direction. But we were on Oor-Rr and while the island certainly had its charms, it was home to neither of us.

I looked back and watched Faith crying. I'd seen her give up before. I'd heard her say she couldn't learn Spanish before she'd even given it a try. I'd heard her dismiss my home and the people there before she'd even had a chance to understand. I'd watched her choose to flee her difficult new situation in a rocket rather than face it. And there on the beach, once again, she was quitting before she'd even begun.

But I'd also seen her try. I'd watched her design a rocket ship when she'd had no idea how to. I'd watched her learn enough Spanish to ask Señor Latas for help. I'd watched her go through model after model after model, and never waver. And I'd watched her bravely face possible annihilation on the day she climbed into a homemade rocket ship and lit the fuse.

As I watched her there snuffling on the sand, I decided she needed help. She needed to be reminded that she was more clever and resourceful than she gave herself credit for, and that physical impossibilities are rare.

I jumped down from the rock and ran along the beach until I found a long, strong stick. I scooped it up in my mouth and trotted over to where Faith and Beverly sat. Faith looked up at me and stopped sobbing. She noticed the stick.

"Not now, Eddie," she said. "No Fetch now, boy." But I wasn't playing.

23
Faith Restored

olding one end of the stick in my mouth, I pushed the other end into the sand a few centimeters.

"What're you doing?" Faith asked.

I dragged the stick along the sand, creating a straight line away from Faith, toward the beach. After two meters or so, I stopped, turned, and dragged the stick away perpendicularly to the line I'd just made.

"Eddie!" Faith said, but I didn't look up from my work.

I made the second line about half as long as the first, then stopped. I lifted the stick up out of the sand, and walked over to the midway point of the first line I'd made. I dug the stick in at this point and began dragging it in the same direction as, and parallel to, the second line. I stopped when the two lines were the same length. Then, I lifted the stick again.

"Why, it's an F!" Beverly said.

"Eddie!" Faith said again, and jumped to her feet.

I wasn't finished.

I dug the stick in again, next to the F, and made a line exactly the same as the tall, vertical line in the F. In fact, in short order I'd made another F right next to the first, to its right (Faith's right, that is).

"Another F!" Beverly said. "By jove, this pooch really has his F's down pat! Did you train him yourself?"

"Eddie!" Faith said again, flabbergasted.

I still wasn't finished.

I sank the stick into the sand one last time, right at the base of the second F's vertical line. I dragged the stick away, parallel to the two horizontal lines above. I stopped when all three horizontal lines were the same length.

"E!" Beverly said.

"What's happening?" Woo-Woof said. "What're you doing, Grumph?"

"Sssshh!" Bark hissed, sensing, I think, something important happening.

Finished, I dropped the stick, sat down beside my letters, and waited for Faith to remember.

"F," she said, "and E. F and E."

"What is it?" Beverly asked. "What does it mean?"

It took her longer than I'd thought it would. I began to worry that she'd forgotten the family tree she'd made with Coco, and the word Coco had taught her.

"*Fe!*" she squealed. "*Fe!*" She hopped up and down with glee. "Is that it, buddy?" she said. "Is that it? My name? *Fe?*"

"Your name is 'Fay'?" Beverly asked.

"In Spanish," Faith said to him. "*Fe,* F-E, means 'faith' in Spanish. You know, like believing in some —"

She stopped dancing.

"What's wrong?" Beverly asked her.

She crouched down before me and looked into my eyes seriously.

"Is that it, Edison?" she said. "Faith? You want me to have faith?"

I nodded.

And she noticed.

24

¡Arriba!

Over the following days, Faith took on the *Peahen*. She banged and bent and cursed and scratched her head and fiddled with her lip and muttered. But she did not quit.

Beverly helped as much as he was able and was good about keeping us all well-fed. In spare moments, he tutored Faith in the fine art of the *tirador,* and she learned quickly.

I spent the time practicing with my stick. I soon had mastered all the letters in the English alphabet and, with Faith's help, began composing words.

"'Dog,'" she'd say. "D-O-G."

And I'd scratch it out in the sand, after which she'd beam and say, "Good boy!"

And then, one afternoon, as I was working on my name, I heard a familiar cry from the cockpit of the *Peahen*.

"Eureka!"

That evening we had a fiesta on the beach, with a bonfire, to celebrate Faith's success. We sang songs and danced, and Beverly cooked *carnitas*. Faith invited Beverly to leave with us in the *Peahen* the next morning, but he graciously declined.

"I think I'll remain," he said, "and see that the electric dogs are well and happy."

Faith smiled and gave him a peck on the cheek, and they both cried.

I explained to the dogs how Faith had repaired the rocket and how we'd be off in the morning.

"Back to Cur-Rr?" Ro-Ro asked.

I realized I didn't really know.

In the morning, we bade our tearful farewells to our new island friends. Beverly gave Faith his *tirador* as a going-away present and Faith gave him her remaining *chicles*. Then she gave each of the electric dogs a hug and a quick belly rub and we climbed into the *Peahen*. She waved to Beverly and the dogs, and then gave a thumbs-up sign.

"T minus two minutes," she said, and ran through her systems check. Once everything was accounted for (minus the *chicles* and the chocolate bars, which she'd devoured long ago), she turned to me.

"It doesn't really matter where you are, does it?" she said with a philosophical look.

I didn't understand.

"I mean," she continued, "wherever you go, there you are, right?"

I nodded but was still a bit unclear on her point.

"All I know is wherever *I* go, there *you* are, buddy," she said, and scratched my head.

I wagged my tail.

"I didn't mean all that about Mexicans," she said. "Sometimes I don't think much."

I smiled.

"Commencing final countdown," she said, "*Diez . . . nueve . . . ocho . . .*"

Spanish!

Siete . . . séis . . . cinco . . . cuatro . . . tres . . . dos . . . uno . . . ¡Vámonos a México! ¡Arriba! ¡Arriba!"

Diez, nueve, ocho, siete, séis, cinco, cuatro, tres, dos, uno
(Spanish): Ten, nine, eight, seven, six, five, four, three, two, one

☆

¡Vámonos a México!
(Spanish): Let's go to Mexico!

☆

¡Arriba! ¡Arriba!
(Spanish): Up! Up!

25
Faith and the Electric Dogs

Our second blast off was just as successful, and just as violent, as the first. Once more we sailed over the ocean blue, over Christmas Island, over Baja California, over Popo. This time, fortunately, we were undisturbed by unfriendly weather conditions and were able to reach our desired destination without calamity. When San Cristóbal de las Casas finally appeared below us, we both cheered.

Faith, who had somehow developed remarkable aviational skills in just two flights (and no landings), set the *Peahen* gently down in a field near the Río Amarillo. We strode through town amidst the festivities of *la posada,* toward El Cerrillo.

When we walked through the door at last, Bernice was there at the kitchen table, crying into her hands. She looked up and saw us, and her face turned beet-red. She screamed and ran at Faith, grabbing her in

la posada
(Spanish): the Mexican festival lasting the nine days before Christmas Day

her arms and hugging her so tightly that Faith's eyes very nearly popped out. She asked a thousand questions, without ever allowing Faith the time or the air to answer, and pelted her daughter's face with tear-soaked kisses. When Hector and Milagros heard the commotion and rushed into the kitchen, they cried and hugged and kissed Faith, too, and then they both scratched my head heartily.

Finally, after the hysteria had died down, Faith told them all about the bone-shaped island and Beverly and the electric dogs. Bernice rolled her eyes, and Hector said, "Oh, *mi hija.*"

When Coco came by that afternoon, she squealed *"¡Fe!"* and then she too cried and hugged and kissed her. She took off the little box necklace and gave it to Faith as a homecoming gift. From that day forward, whenever Coco came to tutor Faith, she found a present waiting for her in Faith's new necklace.

Faith suddenly possessed a whole new attitude about learning Spanish and being in Mexico. She said that she couldn't wait for the holidays to end, and for school to resume.

"I've got a few fishy faces of my own," she told me, and gave a snap on her *tirador.*

Faith spent a great deal of time during the holidays with Milagros, helping her with the cooking and cleaning. Milagros showed Faith how to embroider, and Faith taught Milagros rocketry. They always spoke in Spanish, except those times when Milagros taught Faith some words in Tzotzil or Faith taught Milagros some in English. By the time school started, Faith spoke Spanish much less reluctantly, and not badly at all, really.

Once back at school, she became so admired for her prowess with the *tirador* that many of the boys who had once teased her, including Diego, were suddenly inviting her over to their homes for target practice. She no longer came home in tears. In fact, she came home singing songs:

> *"El maestro,* teacher, *el piso,* floor,
> *La ventana,* window, *la puerta,* door,
> *El lápiz,* pencil, *la pluma,* pen,
> *El gallo,* rooster, *la gallina,* hen."

As for me, dear reader, I spent the time becoming reacquainted with my old pals after persuading Faith to take me out to visit them more often. On rare occasions, we'd invite one or two of them over to the house for kibbles and a demonstration of my new talents in stickmanship. Naturally, this occurred only when Bernice was nowhere to be seen.

And, of course, I continued practicing my writing. I picked up a pencil and practiced on paper. Then I began reading. I started with *Higglety Pigglety Pop!* (after it had dried out), since I knew it by heart, then I read *The Amazing Bone.* Oh, the joy of reading! I had no idea! People really are the luckiest, cleverest creatures.

Very soon, I was writing whole sentences on paper. My written vocabulary grew by leaps and bounds. My desire to learn to write was limitless. I was even more obsessed than I was during my Fetch days.

And then, once my abilities had developed to a level which I felt were suitable for doing so, I wrote a whole story, from beginning to end. A true story, about Faith and me and the electric dogs.

I hope you liked it.

the end

Glossary

All terms in Spanish except where indicated.

Adiós: Good-bye

¡Afuera!: Out!

amiga: female friend

amigos: friends

¡Arriba! ¡Arriba!: Up! Up!

¡Ay caramba!: Oh, my goodness!

¡Ay, perrito!: Oh, little dog!

bock (Bowwow): parrot

¡Bravo!: Bravo!

Buenos días: Good morning

C'est magnifique! (French): It's magnificent!

Cálmate, perrito: Calm down, little dog

carnitas: roasted pork nuggets glazed in fat drippings

chiapaneco: from Chiapas

chicles: chewing gum

¿Cómo?: What?

¿Cómo se dice . . . ?: How do you say . . . ?

¿Cómo se dice "Faith" en español?: How do you say "Faith" in Spanish?

compadres: pals; chums

cur (Bowwow): electric dog

De nada: You're welcome

Dices "Quiero un cohete, por favor": Say "I want a rocket, please"

dicho: saying; proverb

diez, nueve, ocho, siete, séis, cinco, cuatro, tres, dos, uno: ten, nine, eight, seven, six, five, four, three, two, one

El que quiera azul celeste, que le cueste: For whomever wants the sky, the price is high

encantado: enchanted; pleased to meet you

fe: faith

fuff (Bowwow): feathers

gracias: thank you

Grar-ark! (Bowwow): No way!

grouk (Bowwow): roasted

indígenas: native people of a particular place (in this case, Southern Mexico)

la posada: the festival celebrated in Mexico lasting the nine days before Christmas Day

luz: light

madre: mother

maestra: female teacher

manteca: fat

mercado: marketplace

Mi chavi 'naj (Tzotzil): Are you hungry?

mi hija: my daughter; an affectionate name for a
     young girl

mira: look

muchacha: a young woman or girl who is hired as a
     servant; literally, young woman

Mu 'yuk xa (Tzotzil): No more

no: no

No entiendo, señorita: I don't understand, miss

No te preocupes, mi hija: Don't worry, my child

om (Bowwow): light

oor (Bowwow): bone

orugas quemadores: furry black caterpillars that
     sting when touched

padrastro: stepfather

panteón: graveyard; cemetery

¡Perfecto!: Perfect!

pip-pips (Bowwow): slingshots

pobrecita: poor thing (female)

¡Qué lástima!: What a shame!

¡Qué milagro!: What a miracle!

Quieres un ¿qué?: You want what?

rork (Bowwow): pork

rr (Bowwow): land

ru (Bowwow): without

Ruff! (Bowwow): Hey!

Ruff, boo-foo! (Bowwow): Hey, yourself!

señora: ma'am; title for a married woman

sí: yes

Sí, en espanol?: Yes, in Spanish?

tirador: slingshot

tiradores: slingshots

¡Tres pesos por cada papaya!: Three pesos for one papaya!

una perra eléctrica: a female electric dog

un perro corriente: an electric dog

¡Vámonos!: Let's go!

¡Vámonos a México!: Let's go to Mexico!

¿Ya?: Ready yet?

yo: I

Yowr-rr-rr! (Bowwow): Yee-ouch!

zapatos eléctricos: electric shoes

zócalo: a town square